PE

"Now you're going to be absolutely terrific to everyone on this vacation, right?" Elizabeth was stern.

"OK, big sister, OK. Whatever you say." Jessica rolled her blue-green eyes skyward.

Elizabeth folded her arms across her chest. "Say it like you mean it, Jessica."

"Liz, I promise, I really do, that I'll be nice to everyone on the trip. I'm going to be so nice that they're going to give me the bike tripper of the year award." Jessica giggled.

"Jess, if that's true, I wouldn't miss this trip for anything in the world!" A brilliant smile lit up Elizabeth's face.

Jessica matched her twin's smile—two identical rays of sunshine. "Count on it, Liz. This is going to be the best vacation we've ever had!"

Bantam Books in the Sweet Valley High Series
Ask your bookseller for the books you have missed

SWEET VALLEY HIGH
Super Edition

PERFECT SUMMER

Written by
Kate William

Created by
FRANCINE PASCAL

BANTAM BOOKS
TORONTO · NEW YORK · LONDON · SYDNEY · AUCKLAND

RL 6, IL age 12 and up

PERFECT SUMMER
A Bantam Book / August 1985

Sweet Valley High is a trademark of Francine Pascal

Conceived by Francine Pascal

Produced by Cloverdale Press, Inc.,
133 Fifth Avenue, New York, N.Y. 10003

Cover art by James Mathewuse

ISBN 0-553-25072-8

Published simultaneously in the United States and Canada

Bantam Books are published by Bantam Books, Inc. Its trademark, consisting of the words ''Bantam Books'' and the portrayal of a rooster, is Registered in U.S. Patent and Trademark Office and in other countries. Marca Registrada. Bantam Books, Inc., 666 Fifth Avenue, New York, New York 10103.

To Eve Becker

One

"Just two pairs of jeans?" Jessica Wakefield wailed. She was studying the photocopied list in her hand as she stood in the middle of her twin sister, Elizabeth's, room. "How on earth am I going to get through a whole month with just two pairs of pants?"

Elizabeth shook her head and laughed. "Jess, we're going on a bike trip, not to a fashion show."

Jessica tossed her shoulder-length, sun-kissed blond hair. "That just shows how much you know, Liz! Think about all the guys we'll be meeting along the way. I, for one, intend to look my best! I'll take four pairs!" She disappeared into her room for a minute and then returned with her newest jeans, her black Levis, and some red cropped pants. She carelessly tossed them into one of her half-packed saddlebags. She was packing in Elizabeth's room because her own

1

room was such a disaster area that there was no space for her to pack. Also, she knew that if she packed in Elizabeth's room, she might just be able to take a few of her sister's things along, too. With that in mind, she headed straight for her sister's closet.

Elizabeth watched as Jessica selected a pair of pearl-gray, raw-silk slacks and removed them from the hanger. "Hold on a minute, Jess. What do you think you're doing?"

"Well, all *my* good pants are dirty," Jessica explained, suddenly looking very innocent.

"Forget it, little sister," Elizabeth said emphatically. The elder of the twins by four minutes, Elizabeth sometimes felt as if it were more like four years. "Those pants weren't made for a bike trip up the California coast—or anywhere else, for that matter. They'll get ruined before you even have a chance to wear them."

Jessica stared at her twin imploringly.

"No way, Jess. Besides, when we get to our first big uphill, you're going to wish you had packed light."

"Well, I could leave out the bicycle wrenches," Jessica suggested, but she tossed the gray slacks onto her sister's bed, anyway.

Elizabeth picked them up and hung them in her closet. "You won't be sorry, Jessica. In fact, you might just find that you actually like spending a month when you don't worry about how you look all the time." She gave Jessica a playful punch on the arm.

But Jessica didn't smile. "Listen, Liz, it might be funny for you. You've got Todd along on this trip." She was referring to Todd Wilkins, Elizabeth's boyfriend, the lean, handsome star of the Sweet Valley High basketball squad. "But I'm going to be keeping my eyes open for cute guys, and I want to make sure they notice me, too."

"You don't need a hundred different outfits for that, silly," Elizabeth replied, rolling her blue jeans into a compact bundle and neatly tucking them into her left saddlebag. "If I know you, you could easily wind up with a different boyfriend in every town we stay in—regardless of what you pack."

Jessica's face lit up like a Christmas tree. "If that's true, this is going to be a great trip!" she declared.

"And who knows," Elizabeth added. "Barry Cooper might turn out to be someone special, too."

"Chrome Dome's nephew?" Jessica shrugged. "If he's anything like his uncle, forget it."

Mr. Cooper, whose shiny bald head had earned him the nickname "Chrome Dome," was the principal of Sweet Valley High, where the twins were students. Mr. Cooper had told his nephew about the bicycle trip when it was being planned, and Barry had decided to fly in from his

3

hometown in Ohio to join the Sweet Valley group.

Elizabeth slipped a bottle of suntan lotion into the outer pocket of one of her saddlebags. "You never know, Jess. He might just turn out to be Prince Charming."

"Well, if he does, I'm ready," Jessica said. "In fact, I feel ready for just about anything." She threw her arms around her sister in an impulsive hug. "Oh, Liz, this trip is going to be the best adventure!"

Elizabeth returned her twin's hug, and a little shiver of excitement ran up her spine. "You bet it is!" she agreed enthusiastically. But as she went back to her packing, a hint of a frown creased her brow. "Only I have to admit that I'm a little worried about Mr. Collins and Ms. Dalton."

Two of the most popular teachers at Sweet Valley High, Roger Collins and Nora Dalton were going to lead the bicycle trip. When the plans had been made, it had seemed that the handsome, strawberry-blond English teacher and the shy, dark-haired French teacher were very much in love. But shortly after the trip had been arranged, the couple had broken up without explanation. Ms. Dalton had gone back to dating wealthy George Fowler, whose daughter, Lila, a friend of Jessica's, was also going on the trip.

"Mr. Collins seems so down lately," Elizabeth continued. "And Ms. Dalton, too. I just hope it won't be too rough on them, being together all the time."

"I don't think that's going to be Ms. Dalton's biggest problem," Jessica said. She quickly disappeared into the adjoining bathroom, then returned with a first-aid kit.

Elizabeth stared at her sister puzzled. "What do you mean?"

"Lila," Jessica stated succinctly, packing the kit. "She's really got it in for that woman."

Elizabeth nodded slowly. "In a funny way, I understand it. Her father spends so little time with her to begin with. I guess Lila blames Ms. Dalton for taking up even more of his time."

"That's pretty dopey of Lila, if you ask me. It's her father's fault, not Ms. Dalton's. Always too busy wheeling and dealing and playing around with his millions to bother with Lila." Jessica put a spare tire tube and a tire-patch kit into her bag.

"That's for sure," Elizabeth agreed. She shook her head grimly. "I can't understand what someone as terrific as Ms. Dalton sees in a man like that."

"Oh, be serious, Liz." Jessica shot her twin an incredulous glance. "George Fowler may not be the most lovable guy, but he's positively rolling in money. I can certainly understand the attraction."

"Jessica Wakefield, when are you ever going to learn that there are more important things in life than money?"

"Maybe when I have so much of it that I don't have to think about it at all," Jessica replied.

Elizabeth sighed. Identical on the outside, from their dazzling smiles to their perfect size-six figures, she and her twin were as different as a gentle breeze and a whipping wind.

"Well, I just don't think Ms. Dalton's the kind of person who is interested in a man's wallet," Elizabeth said. "And it would be awfully nice if Lila made an effort to get along with her on this trip."

Jessica pictured the look of pure hatred that crossed her friend Lila's face whenever the pretty French teacher was around. "I wouldn't bet on that, Liz. You know, Lila almost backed out of this trip when Ms. Dalton started going out with her father again. In the end, Mr. Fowler pressured her to go. He thinks it'll be a good chance for the two women in his life to get to know each other better. Ha! Now Lila resents Ms. Dalton even more. She says she's ruining her summer plans." Jessica shook her head. "Nope, I wouldn't count on Lila's softening toward Ms. Dalton one single bit. And what's more I wouldn't bet on Bruce's being nice to Roger, either."

"I guess not," Elizabeth said, some of her excitement about the trip dissolving in anxiety. "I wonder if Bruce will ever admit that Roger is every bit as much a Patman as he is."

Roger Patman, born Roger Barrett, had been

as poor as a church mouse most of his sixteen years. But after the death of his mother, some shocking news had been disclosed, surprising Roger—and the rest of a very startled Sweet Valley. Roger Barrett was, in fact, actually Roger Patman, cousin of smug Bruce Patman and heir to a mind-boggling fortune.

"But maybe having Liv along on the trip will take some of the sting out of Bruce's nastiness," Elizabeth said, cheering up at the thought of Olivia Davidson, Roger's longtime girlfriend.

"Right. Miss Artsy-Craftsy Olivia to the rescue," Jessica said.

"Oh, come on, Jess. Liv's a friend of mine."

"So?" Jessica made a face. "We both know that we don't have the same taste in friends. Especially best friends."

Elizabeth threw her sister a dangerously dark glance. "Is that supposed to be another remark about Enid?"

Enid Rollins was Elizabeth's closest friend in the world. She was spending the summer working at Casey's Ice-Cream Parlor in the Valley Mall.

"Liz, don't tell me you're going to get all worked up again over that wimp."

"I certainly am going to get worked up, unless you take back what you said about Enid. And Olivia too."

Jessica was silent.

"I'm giving you exactly one minute." It was

plain to see that Elizabeth meant business. She rarely got angry, but when she did, she could be every bit as tough as her twin.

Jessica noted her sister's clenched fists and tight expression. "Oh, all right, Liz. I guess Enid'll do. And Olivia—well, the truth of the matter is that I don't really feel one way or another about her."

"But you're going to be absolutely terrific to her this vacation, right?" Elizabeth was stern. "And everybody else on the trip, too."

"OK, big sister, OK. Whatever you say." Jessica rolled her blue-green eyes skyward.

Elizabeth folded her arms across her chest. "Say it like you mean it, Jessica."

"Liz, don't look at me like that. I promise, I really do, that I'll be nice to everyone on the trip."

Elizabeth's expression softened. "Sure?"

"Abso-posi-lutely! I'm going to be so nice that they're going to give me the bike tripper of the year award." Jessica giggled.

"Jess, if that's true, I wouldn't miss this trip for anything in the world!" A brilliant smile lit up Elizabeth's face.

Jessica matched her twin's smile—two identical rays of sunshine. "Count on it, Liz. This is going to be the best vacation we've ever had!"

"Has anyone seen my sleeping bag?" Jessica yelled, frantically searching through the

Wakefield living room and under the plush beige sofa.

"Jess, I loaded it into the car already," shouted the twins' brother, Steven, from the front walk. "You'd better hurry if you don't want to be late."

Jessica took one last look around the familiar, comfortably furnished split-level house as she made her way to the door. She felt a funny little pang running through her body.

"Jess, it's all going to be here when you get back, just the way you left it," Steven called, peering in at Jessica through the open front door, a look of amusement in his dark eyes.

"Of course it is!" Jessica snapped, embarrassed to be caught engaging in a moment of sentimentality. "I was just checking to make sure I hadn't left anything," she contended.

"Everything's in the car," Steven replied. "And so are Mom and Dad and Liz. So move it."

"OK, OK, I'm coming," Jessica gave Steven a little frown as she swept down the front walk and pulled open the door of Mr. Wakefield's rust-brown LTD. "All set," she announced, as she climbed into the backseat beside Elizabeth. Steven squeezed in next to her, and Jessica stuck her tongue out at him.

"Practicing to scare all the boys away, Jess?" Steven quipped.

"Steve, why don't you make like a seafood special and just clam up," Jessica shot back.

In the front seat, Alice Wakefield sighed.

"That's one thing I'm not going to miss. All the squabbling." She folded her sun-bronzed arms across her trim, lithe frame. It was easy to see that the twins got their all-American good looks from their fair-haired, blue-eyed mother.

"I don't know about that, Alice," Ned Wakefield put in as he started the car. "It's going to be awfully quiet around here without Liz and Jessica's arguing over their bathroom every morning." His brown eyes twinkled mischievously.

Elizabeth laughed. "I'm sure Jess and I could call you up once in a while and argue on the phone!"

Ned Wakefield laughed along with his daughter. "Thanks, but no thanks, Liz. It's not going to be *that* quiet. I hear that college boys home on summer vacation can make quite a racket!" He steered the car through the rolling hills of Sweet Valley, which were carpeted with lush grass and colorful patches of fragrant summer flowers.

"I'll try my best," Steven joked.

As they rounded a bend in the road, the spacious, tree-dotted lawn of Sweet Valley High came into view. Mr. Wakefield pulled through the campus gates and came to a stop in front of the pillared entrance to the school building. Around the front steps, a half-dozen or so of the twins' classmates were gathered, bicycles loaded, smiles of excitement and nervous anticipation on their faces. Parents and relatives milled around, too, and from the car window, Jessica could see George Fowler standing very close to Nora Dalton. Lila's back was to them, as she bent over her top-of-the-line, super-fancy bicycle.

"Well, this is it," Alice Wakefield said as the family got out of the car and began unloading the twins' bicycles from the roof rack.

Jessica felt her pulse racing as she scanned the group of people. Olivia Davidson and Annie Whitman sat under a tree with Olivia's mother and Mrs. Whitman, whose arm was around her daughter's shoulders. Handsome Roger Collins stood at one side of the group, opposite Nora Dalton, talking to Charlie Markus, Bruce Patman's friend from the tennis team, who was also going on the trip.

Behind the Wakefields, a green Ford sedan had pulled up, and Todd Wilkins jumped out, his wavy brown hair flopping over one eye as he ran over to Elizabeth and planted a big kiss on her lips. Neither Roger nor Bruce Patman had arrived yet, nor had the mysterious Barry Cooper.

Jessica fastened her two saddlebags on each side of her rear bike rack and secured her sleeping bag on top of it with an elastic shock cord. She waited impatiently until Todd and Elizabeth had finished their hello kisses, and then the three of them joined the rest of the group, Alice and Ned Wakefield, Steven, and Todd's parents behind them.

A few minutes later a long black limousine pulled up, and Roger and Bruce piled out. Bruce was clearly doing his best to ignore his cousin, but if Roger was fazed by it, he didn't show it. He was all smiles as Olivia ran over to him and gave him a big hug.

Henry Wilson Patman emerged from the limousine behind Bruce and Roger and cast an icy look in the direction of George Fowler, his longtime adversary. After the chauffeur had unloaded the bicycles, Mr. Patman shook hands with his son and nephew and solemnly climbed back into the cavernous depths of the huge car.

"I wonder where Mrs. Patman was?" commented Elizabeth as the limousine pulled away and disappeared out of the Sweet Valley High gates.

"Off having her hair styled or her nails manicured, or perhaps she's on a weekend shopping trip in Paris," Jessica answered, not without a hint of jealousy.

"Jess," Elizabeth said with mock consternation, "would you rather be in some stuffy department store, spending money that someone else earned, or on a real, live adventure like the one you're about to be on?"

"We-e-ell . . ." Jessica hedged. But any further discussion was cut short by the arrival of Chrome Dome Cooper's brown Dodge Dart.

"Here he is!" exclaimed Lila, coming up behind Jessica for a clear view of Barry Cooper. "I bet he's gorgeous!"

The entire group watched, as the front passenger door opened. All eyes were on the pudgy, pale-faced boy who waddled out.

"Oh, no." Jessica groaned.

"Brother, you said it," Lila agreed. "What a loser!"

Barry tried to heave his saddlebags from the trunk of his uncle's car, his face becoming red with the effort. But as soon as he had lifted them out, they slipped from his grasp, falling on the ground—and on his right foot. "Ow-w," Barry moaned.

From the back of the crowd, Bruce Patman snickered.

"Well, Liz, so much for Prince Charming," Jessica said to her twin. "Seems more like a toad to me."

Elizabeth felt a sinking sensation in the pit of her stomach. She suspected that Mr. Cooper's roly-poly nephew had come all the way from Ohio for a whopping big dose of trouble.

But Elizabeth's concern about Barry Cooper was soon forgotten in the flurry of high-spirited goodbyes and last-minute pre-trip jitters.

"Don't forget to write, kitten," Mrs. Whitman told Annie as she hugged her tightly. George Fowler gave Nora Dalton one last kiss as Lila pouted and Roger Collins looked away.

"You guys have a great time," Steven instructed his sisters after Alice and Ned Wakefield had bid their daughters farewell.

Finally, all the well-wishers were gone. Only twelve people remained. Elizabeth looked around her. For four whole weeks—and for better or worse—it was just them, their bicycles, and the hundreds of miles of California coast that stretched ahead of them.

Two

"Dear Enid," Elizabeth wrote to her best friend:

We made camp at our first stop yesterday, at campgrounds near a little town on Newport Bay. It was a new experience for a lot of us—learning how to set up tents, helping to build a camp fire, and cooking out our first dinner. We rotate jobs every day—cooking, cleaning up after meals, buying supplies, and so forth—and Olivia and I were assigned to prepare the first meal. Enid, you should have seen us trying to cook an individual chicken-parmigiana cutlet for everyone in the group! Next time we'll know to stick to something really simple, like hot dogs!

Amazingly enough, everyone seems to be on his or her best behavior so far. Lila Fowler actually got down on her hands and knees in the dirt to get the fire started, and Jessica did just as thorough a job of making sure it was extinguished properly at the end of the evening. (Mr. Collins gave us a lecture about forest fires and told us that there was a real problem this year because of the drought we've had.) Bruce got stuck cleaning pots, but to everyone's shock, he barely uttered a word of complaint. I guess I'd better enjoy his cooperation while it lasts!

The first day of cycling was kind of tough. To begin with, I didn't have any idea how hard it would be to ride a fully loaded bike. In addition to our own things, we each have to carry a share of the group equipment—a two-person tent, or cookware, or canned food, and so on. I guess when I was doing my practice rides before the trip, I should have tried cycling with a loaded bicycle. Roger and Olivia did, and it really showed— they were always out in front of the group. Of course Bruce couldn't bear to be outdone by Roger, so he was up in front, too, though his huffing and puffing gave away the fact that he hadn't done any biking at all before the trip. I guess cycling muscles and tennis muscles aren't necessarily the same ones.

Then at the other end of the pack was poor Barry Cooper, Mr. Cooper's nephew.

Elizabeth put down her pen for a moment and

sighed. Around her the rest of the group was waking up. Kids were peeking out of the tents or heading for the campground washing facilities, toothbrushes, bars of soap, and towels in hand.

Barry Cooper had just emerged from the tent he had shared with Mr. Collins and was trying, without much luck, to stuff his sleeping bag—as bulky and inappropriate for camping as Barry himself was—into a sack made for a much sleeker kind of sleeping bag. Elizabeth shook her head and picked up her pen again.

Enid, I wish I could tell you that Barry fits right in with the Sweet Valley kids, but nothing could be further from the truth. I've already found myself defending him several times against nasty remarks, and I'm afraid this may be only the beginning. Nothing seems to go right for Barry. He lags way behind the rest of us when we're riding, and he manages to mess up even the simplest chores. What's worse, he seems to have taken a liking to Jessica! As you can imagine, my sister isn't terribly thrilled about the whole thing.

Another crush that seems to be developing is on the part of Charlie Markus, Bruce's tennis teammate. I keep seeing him sneaking sidelong looks at Annie Whitman when he thinks no one else is watching. Annie, on the other hand, has been paying more attention to the scenery than to Charlie's advances. Maybe her breakup with Ricky Capaldo is still too recent for her to think about a new boy, even though she and Ricky came out of it with their friendship very much intact.

But, Enid, I'm getting off the subject. And besides, Annie does have every reason to be taken with the scenery. The roads weave through forests of cedar, pine, and eucalyptus and come out onto sandstone bluffs with striking views of the ocean crashing against the shore. Our campground, too, is nestled in a pine grove not far from the beach. It's spectacular—and so romantic, too. I feel lucky to be able to share all this natural beauty with someone as special as Todd.

Elizabeth paused and looked toward Todd's tent. He and Roger were already taking the stakes out of the ground and preparing to roll the tent up. She caught Todd's eye, and he blew her a kiss. She continued to write.

Other notes of romance are as follows: Jessica and Lila have already befriended two boys whom they met on the beach yesterday, but when we get back on the road this morning, the guys will be left in the dust—or the wind, is more like it. Not that either Jess or Lila really seems to mind. As

Jessica said to me, "Why get stuck on one when there are so many others out there, just waiting for me to ride along!" Well, you know my sister!

On a more serious note, though, the only real problem is between Mr. Collins and Ms. Dalton. They're trying not to show it, but things are strained between them. Fortunately, they take turns riding at the back of the group to make sure everyone is OK (read, *Barry* is OK), so they don't have to cycle together. And yesterday, Mr. Collins went to the beach with Jessica, Lila, and Bruce while the rest of us did some sightseeing. (We went to a really neat eighteenth-century mission built by the Spaniards when the West was just being settled.)

Anyway, I do hope things improve between those two. The best thing that could happen would be for them to take a little of their own advice. The first day of our trip, they told us that this vacation was a time to put away old grudges and gripes and to start fresh. I think this was a hint to Bruce and Roger. Or maybe it was Ms. Dalton's way of suggesting a truce between herself and Lila. But it's also the soundest advice our trip leaders could give themselves. I hope they think about that.

Otherwise, everything's terrific. Today we leave for Los Angeles, where we'll stay with the Thomases, friends of the Patmans', for three days. Mr. Thomas is a big-deal Hollywood agent, and his mansion is supposed to be fit for a king! Then we leave luxury behind. The rest of the trip is scheduled for campgrounds and youth hostels, with two phantom days—that is, days where it's up to us to find our own accommodations. We'll have to follow some rules at the hostels (curfews, checkout times, for example), but Mr. Collins says that we'll appreciate having kitchen facilities and real beds. Also, it will be a good opportunity to meet kids on other bike trips, which, as you can guess, pleases Jessica and Lila immensely.

Hope everything is going well in Sweet Valley and you're not too tired of making hot-fudge sundaes yet. I miss you.

Love,
Liz

Elizabeth reread her letter. A reporter for *The Oracle*, the Sweet Valley High newspaper, and writer of its weekly gossip column, as well as the author of dozens of stories and poems that she had hidden in her drawer at home, Elizabeth viewed absolutely everything she wrote with a critical eye. Jessica liked to joke that even Elizabeth's shopping list had to be a masterpiece.

She picked up her pen and added one more sentence. ''P.S. Whatever happens on this adventure, I'm ready for it." Satisfied, she folded the letter and put it in its envelope.

As it turned out, Elizabeth wasn't at all ready for Courtney Thomas. Courtney was the daughter of the Patmans' friend, Steve Thomas, who had offered the group the use of the grounds of his Los Angeles estate. Elizabeth had her first glimpse of Courtney the following afternoon, after another hard day of cycling and muscles that were even more sore than they'd been the previous day.

"I may never ride again," Elizabeth joked wryly as she got off her bicycle in front of the impressive wrought-iron gates that led to the Thomas mansion.

"I know how you feel, Liz," Ms. Dalton sympathized, "but this is the worst of it. I promise. Now that our bodies are getting used to the cycling, it's going to be easier."

"Or at least for as long as we're in Los Angeles," kidded Olivia. "Bruce, hurry up and announce our arrival!"

Bruce got off his bicycle and swaggered up to the gate house. "Can you tell Mr. Thomas that Bruce Patman and company are here?" he asked the gatekeeper. Actually, Elizabeth mused, the way Bruce said it, it sounded more like an order than a request.

A few minutes later, the group was being welcomed by tall, handsome Steve Thomas, a big-time agent for a host of Hollywood stars. With his bright, broad smile, his rich, melodious voice, and his outgoing theatrical manner, Mr. Thomas seemed as if he himself could have been a star.

"Bruce, my boy," he boomed out, "how marvelous to see you again." He gave Bruce a hearty handshake with one hand, while he clapped him on the back with the other. "And Roger. Hello, son. And this must be the Sweet Valley bicycle group I've heard so much about. Welcome, welcome to my home. I'm delighted to have you stay with us. With my daughter, Courtney, and me, that is. It's just the two of us. Oh, and Courtney's so eager to meet all of you. She's out by the pool, waiting right now. Why don't you come and say hello to her?"

The twelve cyclists pushed their bicycles up the winding driveway, past perfectly manicured hedges and floral gardens, two clay tennis courts, and a huge glass-and-redwood bathhouse. Mr. Thomas, who kept up a nearly constant monologue as he led them across the grounds, explained that behind the bathhouse was an outdoor courtyard with an eight-person Jacuzzi hot tub.

"Of course, you're all welcome to try it out," he offered as the group came around the other side of the bathhouse to a vast expanse of green grass. In front of them was an oversize, kidney-shaped swimming pool complete with diving boards and a water slide. By the side of the pool, lounging in a deck chair and sipping an ice-filled drink, was a girl of about the twins' age, with tumbling, jet-black curls and a deep bronze tan, tall and trim in an ultrafashionable one-piece black tank suit.

"Courtney, precious," called Mr. Thomas. "You remember Mr. and Mrs. Patman, don't you? Well, this is their son, Bruce, and their nephew, Roger. And these are all their wonderful friends."

Courtney removed her sunglasses, her almond-shaped eyes surveying each member of the group in turn. As her gaze swept over the last person—Barry Cooper, standing off to one side of the others—she put her dark glasses back on and returned to her drink without so much as a hello or even a nod.

"Well, la-di-da," muttered Jessica, standing by Elizabeth's side.

"Courtney, dear," said Mr. Thomas, "why don't you show our guests where they can pitch their tents?"

Courtney's only response was to toss her black curls, disdain etched on her perfect features.

"Come on now, darling," Mr. Thomas cajoled. "Be a good hostess for me, OK?" He hid his embarrassment at his daughter's behavior behind a hearty laugh.

Courtney took her time getting up, stretching

23

her arms and her long, tanned legs, then swiveling around so her feet touched the ground. As she pulled herself up out of her chair, she sighed as if it were the biggest imposition in the world.

"That's my girl," Steve Thomas said with obvious relief.

Courtney set out across the grass, never looking back at the Sweet Valley contingent as they pushed their bicycles past the pool and up a gentle slope. Mr. Thomas followed at the rear of the procession, talking animatedly to Nora Dalton and Roger Collins.

As Courtney led the procession down the other side of the incline, the yard in front of the estate came into view—a thick carpet of green with a crystal-clear stream running along a rock bed at the side of the mansion. The mansion itself seemed to stretch on forever, a redwood-and-glass masterpiece in the same style as the bathhouse.

"Here's where you can put your tents up," Courtney muttered, giving a curt wave of her hand, her blood-red polished fingernails glinting in the late afternoon sunlight.

"You people make yourselves comfortable," Steve Thomas added more graciously. His voice was bright and cheerful. Almost too cheerful, Elizabeth thought, as if he were making up for his daughter's rudeness.

"And if you need anything, just come knock on the door and ask me. Or ask Court—"

His words were cut short by the roar of a dirt bike coming over the hill and straight toward them. Mr. Thomas's cheerful posture slipped away like fine sand escaping through a sieve. He could no longer force a smile. His face clouded over, and frown lines appeared on his forehead and around his mouth. Courtney, on the other hand, suddenly came alive.

"Nolan!" she cried, waving her arms above her head.

"Courtney, dear, I thought we had decided that you weren't going to see him anymore." Steve Thomas's voice was low but stern.

Courtney, however, came on loud and clear. "Maybe *you* decided that, Daddy, dear," she retorted. "But I wouldn't ever be so foolish as to agree to giving up Nolan. Compared to him, every other boy I've ever known is dull, dull, dull."

As the bike got closer, leaving churned-up bits of grass and dirt in its wake, Elizabeth could make out its rider—dressed from head to toe in black leather. He was wearing spike-studded wristbands and calf-high, black, lace-up army boots he had decorated with heavy chains. His hair was shorn almost to his skull, except for a narrow strip that ran from the middle of his forehead to his neck and stood straight up in stiff bristles.

He rode at top speed, right toward the Sweet Valley crowd, stopping only at the last second.

"Well, well. What do we have here? A bunch of good little girls and boys. Hoping maybe some of it'll rub off on Courtney, Mr. T?" Nolan's voice was heavy with sarcasm.

"You've got his number, Nolan." Courtney snickered, apparently not at all ashamed to treat her father so shabbily in front of guests. "But don't worry about my buying the goody-goody number. Just the thought of it puts me right to sleep."

"For God's sake, Courtney, not now," Mr. Thomas implored. "Please."

His daughter ignored him. "Me," she added, "I go where the action is." She swung one leg over the back of Nolan's bike, getting seated as he peeled away from the small crowd, churning up the lawn as he went.

Steve Thomas raced after his daughter and Nolan. "You come back here right this instant," he shouted. "Courtney! Nolan, I warn you. . . ." But the motorcycle got farther and farther away, until Courtney, clad in nothing but her skimpy bathing suit, was no more than a tiny speck on the horizon.

Mr. Thomas flung his hands up in frustration and embarrassment. "I'm so sorry. Courtney— well, she just hasn't been herself lately," he apologized lamely.

The image stuck in Elizabeth's mind as she

and Annie set up the tent they'd share for the next three days: bubbly Mr. Thomas reduced to making excuses for his daughter as she rode off with her warped version of Prince Charming. The image stayed with her as she and Todd lounged around the pool later with a few of the other kids, enjoying the sunset over the beautifully kept grounds.

"Mr. Thomas may be one of the best agents in Hollywood," Elizabeth remarked to her boyfriend, "and he's definitely a first-rate host, but it looks like he's got a whopper of a problem when it comes to his daughter."

"Yeah, I know what you mean," Todd agreed. "I couldn't believe that show she put on for us earlier."

"Poor Mr. Thomas. I feel sorry for him," Elizabeth commented, dangling her feet in the pool. "And for her, too. Deep down she must be pretty miserable if she has to act like that."

"Oh, I wouldn't feel sorry for her," Todd said. "She lives in this paradise with every imaginable luxury." He gestured to the magnificent grounds and house. "If she's not satisfied," added Todd, "it's because she's spoiled rotten. Beautiful, but as spoiled as they come."

Elizabeth gave Todd a sidelong glance. "Beautiful, huh?"

"Well, she would be if she didn't have such a foul personality," Todd amended.

"Oh, come on, Todd." Elizabeth laughed. "You can be bad and beautiful at the same time."

"OK, OK. You win, Liz. I admit it. I think the girl's beautiful. But I know someone who's even more beautiful." Todd leaned toward Elizabeth and cupped her face in his large, strong hands.

She met his loving, brown-eyed gaze, and their lips met in a sweet, lingering kiss. Elizabeth forgot Courtney. At that moment, there wasn't a shadow of a doubt in her mind who was number one in Todd's book.

Elizabeth might have tossed all thoughts of Courtney to the wind, but the rebellious, sharp-tongued girl was never far from Mr. Thomas's mind.

The day after the Sweet Valley group had arrived, Mr. Thomas had insisted that Courtney take them around town, imposing his decision by threatening to cut off her allowance, disconnect her private telephone, and take away her charge privileges.

He'd managed to have his way, but as the group was enjoying lunch at a Mexican restaurant down by the water, Courtney had excused herself to make a telephone call. Ten minutes later, just as the main courses were arriving, Nolan Ruggers had shown up on his motorbike and whisked Courtney away.

The Sweet Valley group assured Courtney's

father that Courtney's desertion had in no way put a damper on their day in Los Angeles. But Steve Thomas was at the end of his rope. No matter what measures he took, his daughter always seemed to end up on the back of Nolan's motorcycle. There had to be a way to stop it.

With that in mind, Mr. Thomas invited Roger Collins and Nora Dalton to the mansion for a cocktail later that evening, while the kids were out getting a taste of Los Angeles's glittery nightlife.

"Ever since she's met Nolan Ruggers, she's been impossible to control," he said as he poured a glass of chilled champagne for Ms. Dalton and fixed a Perrier with lime for Mr. Collins. "I've tried everything, but she seems to get tremendous satisfaction out of breaking all the rules I make and flinging her disregard for me in my face." He sighed and helped himself to a Perrier. "The more time she spends with that terrible boy, the worse she gets. Sometimes I don't have the strength left to fight with her anymore."

Roger Collins nodded politely. He felt mildly uncomfortable, listening to the family problems of a man he barely knew, and being in the same room with Nora Dalton didn't help. Things were so strained between them, he felt sure that Steve Thomas must be aware of it.

But Steve Thomas had his own problems, and he quickly got to the point of the meeting in the study. "When you people came to stay yesterday," he declared, "I suddenly saw a ray of hope for Courtney. Those kids are a terrific bunch. The spirit, the group cooperation—I'm really impressed. And they seem to be having a great time." He took a sip of his Perrier. "Well, I thought, that's exactly what Courtney needs. Nolan was right, you know, about my hoping the influence of your group might do Courtney some good. And I refuse to believe that it won't work. She could discover that excitement doesn't have to be a delinquent on a motorbike."

Roger Collins stroked his chin and thought out loud. "I suppose we *could* take turns sleeping three in a tent—although our reservations at the youth hostels were made for a group of twelve."

"I could have my secretary call the hostels to make arrangements for one extra person," Mr. Thomas put in quickly. "Please say you'll take her. Next month I've arranged to send her to her aunt in New Mexico. But until then. . . . You've got to take her. You must." His voice took on an edge of desperation. "Look, I'll level with you. This boy, Nolan Ruggers—he's a big troublemaker. I hear he's into all kinds of things—drugs, petty thievery. Last year he was hauled down to the police station for holding up a grocery store, although he got off on some technicality or other. Roger, Nora—I'm scared stiff about Courtney. Who knows what Nolan's been convincing her to do. This trip—it could be her salvation. And mine."

Roger Collins weighed the pros and cons of taking Courtney along. He found himself thinking that perhaps Steve Thomas had given up on disciplining his daughter and that he was now turning to someone else for a solution. What's more, there were certainly more pleasant prospects than suddenly becoming responsible for a girl like Courtney.

On the other hand it would clearly be best to get Courtney as far away from Nolan Ruggers as possible. And no matter what shortcomings Steve Thomas might have had in disciplining his daughter, he had been an exemplary host—as generous and wonderful as possible. If he thought Courtney could benefit from the bicycle trip, the least they could do would be to make her welcome.

But it was Nora Dalton who made the final decision. "If everything you say is true, Steve, I don't see how we can refuse you."

Roger Collins nodded. "You tell Courtney," the handsome English teacher said to Mr. Thomas. "As soon as the others get back tonight, Nora and I will let them know that Courtney is now officially part of the group."

Three

The next morning, Courtney approached the spot where the tents were pitched to invite the group to the house for breakfast. Gone was the frostiness of the previous two days. The sultry pout had been replaced by a toothpaste-commercial smile. In the blink of an eye, Courtney had somehow miraculously become a totally new person. And that was when all Elizabeth's troubles began.

"I had our housekeeper bake a batch of fresh blueberry muffins," she said, beaming proudly as if she had made them with her very own hands. "And since Daddy's out with a client, I need some help eating them. I thought since we're going to be together for the rest of the month, we might as well start getting to know each other now."

Was it Elizabeth's imagination, or did Courtney look right at Todd as she spoke? She immediately extinguished her ember of suspicion before it flared into a fire of jealousy. She was too secure in Todd's love, she told herself, for even an instant of doubt. Besides, right now most of her energy was channeled into utter amazement at the one-hundred-and-eighty-degree turnaround in Courtney.

"I know we didn't get off to the best start," Courtney was saying to the group, "and I apologize for that. Everyone has a few bad days every once in a while, right?" she asked simply. Her silver laugh floated across the lush green lawn. "But I'm going to start making up for that, right here and now," she added.

Incredible, Elizabeth thought to herself. *Is it really possible for someone to change overnight like that?*

Jessica seemed to be of the same mind, although she put it a little differently. "She isn't going to pull the wool over *my* eyes," she said to Elizabeth as the Sweet Valley group followed Courtney up to the huge house for breakfast. "I don't know what kind of stunt she's planning, but she's not going to convince me with that sweetness-and-light act." Jessica shook her head vigorously. "She can stuff us full of all the muffins she wants to, but there's no way I'm forgiving her for what she said about us the other day. Nobody calls me a goody-goody and gets away with it."

"Me neither," echoed Lila Fowler, who trailed

along next to Elizabeth and Jessica behind the rest of the group.

Elizabeth laughed. "You two act as if being called a goody-goody is the worst thing in the world."

"Maybe for people like you it's not," Jessica returned seriously. "But for us . . ."

A twinkle came into Elizabeth's eye. "I think I've just been insulted," she said lightly. "In fact, I think my own twin has just insinuated that I, Elizabeth Wakefield, am a goody-goody."

Jessica didn't join in her sister's laughter. "Liz, you might think this whole thing is a joke, but that girl just assumes she can be as horrible as she likes and that we'll all forgive her the moment she smiles. Are you going to let her get away with that?"

Elizabeth glanced at Courtney, talking animatedly with Todd as she headed the procession. Todd didn't seem to mind her attention a bit. "I don't know, Jess," she replied slowly. "I certainly hope Courtney's intentions are good. This sudden switch seems almost impossible. Still, I guess only time will tell."

As for the others, they seemed a bit hesitant about Courtney's new attitude, but as the morning wore on, they became more receptive to their hostess. Over breakfast, she and Bruce traded stories about traveling in Europe. Annie told her all about the town of Sweet Valley, and Courtney appeared to be properly captivated.

Most of the kids began softening toward her. And at that point she decided to take them into her confidence. Or at least it appeared that way at the time.

"You know it was really my father's idea that I come on this trip," Courtney told them, buttering a warm muffin, "and I can't say I'm thrilled about roughing it. But maybe with you people it won't be so bad." She looked straight at Todd as she spoke. This time Elizabeth was certain.

"Well, if you need any help with anything, just speak up," Todd volunteered. "We'll be happy to give you a hand." His brown eyes crinkled at the corners as he gave a friendly smile.

"I might take you up on your offer," Courtney said. "You know, the closest I've ever come to camping out was during a vacation in Austria, when the plumbing in my hotel room went on the blink and I had to share the public bathroom at the end of the hall." She gave her silvery laugh again, as if she had told the funniest joke in the world.

"Poor little rich girl," Jessica muttered to Elizabeth.

"No, I'm definitely not used to roughing it," Courtney continued cheerfully. "In fact, that's why my father insisted I come on this trip in the first place. To toughen up!"

Across the lace-covered dining-room table, Elizabeth caught Roger Collins and Nora Dalton

35

giving each other a funny look. It was the first glance they'd exchanged since the trip had started, so Elizabeth found it hard to brush her observation away. Did the two trip leaders know something about Courtney that they weren't telling?

Mr. Collins looked as if he was about to say something, but when Ms. Dalton gave a tiny, almost imperceptible shake of her head, he shut his mouth.

Elizabeth turned all this over in her mind. She had a feeling that somehow, the new Courtney and this silent interchange between Mr. Collins and Ms. Dalton were parts of a larger puzzle. But she didn't have the first clue as to how to begin fitting the pieces together.

She was still pondering this after breakfast as she and the others got ready for a day at Los Angeles's biggest playground, Disneyland.

"Boy, this is going to be great!" Todd's voice broke into her thoughts.

"Mm, yeah, it is," she replied distractedly, folding a light sweater and putting on her day pack.

"Sure is nice of Courtney to offer to take us around there, isn't it?" he continued. "I guess she's not so bad after all, huh?"

Elizabeth snapped out of her reverie and looked straight into her boyfriend's brown eyes. "Todd," she began, "don't you think Courtney's instant change in attitude is a little strange?"

Todd shrugged. "I guess it is. I mean, yes, sure it is. Everyone thinks so, but—well, I figure Courtney realized she was stuck with us for the trip and that she was going to have to start shaping up if she didn't want to have a rotten time."

Elizabeth's blue-green eyes remained clouded with disbelief. "Weren't you the one who said Courtney was spoiled rotten?" she asked.

"Liz, you've got to give people the benefit of the doubt." His voice took on a note of reproof. "I learned that from you, remember."

Elizabeth sighed. "How can I argue with you? According to Jessica, giving people the benefit of the doubt is my motto. And she doesn't mean it as a compliment."

"Then she's got something to learn," Todd said emphatically. "I think it's the only fair thing to do."

"You're right," Elizabeth replied. "But I just can't shake the feeling that something is going on. First that horrible guy, Nolan, and Courtney not acting too much better herself, then the two of them leaving us at that restaurant, and now, suddenly he seems to have disappeared and she's become an absolute angel."

"Liz," Todd began as they walked toward one of the two black limousines that Mr. Thomas had furnished for their trip to Disneyland. "You can either drive yourself nuts trying to figure out Courtney's new way of looking at things, or you

37

can just accept the fact that she's now opening herself up to us, and respond like a friend."

But it was easier said than done. There was no way that Elizabeth could ignore the fact that Courtney managed to sit next to Todd on most of the scary rides. Or that when they went through the Haunted Mansion, she squealed and held on to him as if for dear life.

It wasn't that Todd encouraged her; he was simply his usual pleasant self. But Elizabeth couldn't help thinking that he could have made more of an effort to include her in the fun.

Jessica wasn't that excited about having Courtney around either. "What do you say we put her on that ride over there—the Matterhorn." Jessica pointed to what looked like an enormous snowcapped mountain. Inside, in pitch darkness, was Disneyland's most frightening roller coaster. "And leave her there for good!" she added.

Elizabeth tried her hardest to be fair, the way she'd promised Todd she would. "Jess, how can you say that? You barely even know the girl."

"Liz, don't tell me you're any fonder of her than I am." Jessica folded her arms across her chest and met her sister's gaze straight on. "Look at her, throwing herself all over your boyfriend."

Elizabeth lowered her head. This was one time when she couldn't disagree with how her sister felt about someone. Elizabeth couldn't bring herself to say anything but what she really felt. "I guess I'd almost prefer the old Courtney to—to this." She gestured helplessly to where Courtney stood, explaining something about the Walt Disney characters to Todd.

"Ah-hah!" Jessica cried triumphantly.

Somehow it didn't make Elizabeth feel any better. Her relief came only when the group finally left Disneyland—earlier than they'd planned because Barry had gotten sick on one of the rides. Poor Barry was red-faced with humiliation, though he tried to pretend that he didn't hear Bruce's snide comments or the snickers of some of the others. But if one good thing came of it, thought Elizabeth, it was that they were headed back to the Thomas estate without Courtney.

She'd ordered a taxi to take her to a friend's house when the group left the amusement park. "I want to say goodbye to someone before we leave," Courtney explained.

Elizabeth wondered if that someone could be Nolan Ruggers. Where *did* he fit into this complicated puzzle anyway? What kind of game was Courtney playing?

No! Stop! Elizabeth chastised herself sharply. She had no right to suspect all sorts of bad things about a girl she'd just met. By sheer force of will, she pushed away the image of Courtney's almond-eyed face and concentrated on Todd's nearness as she snuggled against him in the leather interior of the limousine. He planted a soft kiss on Elizabeth's forehead, and she smiled.

Elizabeth's happiness was short-lived. Mr. Thomas had planned a send-off dinner on the deck of the mansion, so a few hours later, Elizabeth was again faced with the reality of Courtney's tinkly laugh and her not-so-subtle overtures to Todd.

The princess held court at the head of a long polished oak table under a latticework canopy blanketed with grapevines. She was swathed in an exotic Indian silk sari, shot through with gold threads. Her hair was gathered loosely off her face, but a few stray black curls cascaded softly down around her shoulders. To complete her outfit, a pair of crescent-shaped hammered-gold earrings dangled from Courtney's ears.

By comparison, Jessica and Lila seemed ordinary in the outfits they were wearing. They sat sullenly while Courtney spun tales of Hollywood's glitterati.

Most of the others, however, including Todd, were awestruck. And Elizabeth could hardly blame them. The names that rolled off Courtney's tongue would have impressed anyone. Actors, producers—she talked about a dazzling array of celebrities as naturally as if they were the people next door, which, Elizabeth reminded herself, they probably were.

"You mean you really know all those stars?" Annie Whitman asked, wide-eyed.

"Sure." Courtney gave an offhanded wave. "When you get down to it, they're just people like you and me. More cider, anyone? Todd?" She refilled his crystal goblet, flashing him a glamorous smile. "Although being famous does have its differences," she said knowingly, embarking on another round of Beverly Hills stories.

As Courtney described a prince's visit to one of her movie-star neighbors, Elizabeth and the others feasted on a first course of sweet, ripe melon and strips of prosciutto, followed by delicate cream of tomato soup.

"Some change from burned, canned-beef stew, huh, gang?" Roger Collins declared when the main course—a sumptuous trout almondine served with fresh asparagus and a spicy shredded carrot salad—was brought out.

Charlie and Bruce grinned sheepishly. The dinner they had made the night before they'd arrived in Los Angeles had not been well received. In fact, Jessica had suggested taking them off cooking duty for good.

Now, at the end of the table, Courtney wrinkled her perfect little nose. "You mean we're going to be eating canned stew?" she said distastefully.

Suddenly Jessica became the biggest defender

of Bruce and Charlie's meal. "Oh, it's not all that horrible, Courtney," she said.

Elizabeth heard more than a trace of annoyance in her twin's words. Clearly Jessica didn't intend to make things easy for Courtney.

"You'd be surprised how good it tastes after you've worked up a real appetite," Jessica continued. "But I guess that wouldn't happen sitting around a pool all day or riding on the back of a motorcycle."

A lightning flash of anger shot across the other girl's face, and for the briefest moment, the old Courtney was back. "Maybe dinner from a can is good enough for *you*, Jessica." She gave a regal toss of her head, but suddenly, she seemed to rein herself in. "What I mean," she amended, softening her tone, a smile touching her lips again, "is that if it's good enough for you, it must be good enough for me. I guess it's just one of the new things I'm going to have to get used to on this trip."

"That's my girl," Steve Thomas said from the other end of the table. His radiant smile throughout dinner was clearly due to Courtney's much improved behavior. He congratulated himself that the mere prospect of the trip seemed to be enough to have wrought such a change in his daughter. True, she had fought like a demon not to be sent with the Sweet Valley group, but once he'd made it plain that it would be impossible to sway his decision, Courtney had adjusted to the

42

idea with a grace that had both surprised and delighted him.

"Besides, Courtney," put in Roger Patman, "just think how good a meal like this will taste after three weeks of bike-trip food."

Courtney nodded. "Yes, I'm sure *all* the pleasures of home will be even more tempting after living on the road." She stressed the word "all," with a funny half-smile that Elizabeth couldn't quite figure out.

Dinner was capped by an assortment of flaky fruit pastries and rich fudge brownies.

"Because my Courtney doesn't think any dinner is complete without chocolate," Mr. Thomas explained, once again beaming at the new, improved Courtney.

Courtney put one of the brownies on her dessert plate and then delicately licked the frosting from her fingertips.

"Well, Courtney's a smart girl," Todd said, reaching for a brownie himself. "I agree with her." He caught Courtney's gaze and gave her a pleasant smile.

She smiled back—a slow, private smile that made Elizabeth's blood run cold. Elizabeth was silent for the remainder of the meal, except at the very end, when she politely thanked Mr. Thomas for dinner.

"Hey, Liz," said Todd as they were walking back to their tents afterward. "Is anything wrong?"

43

"Why do you ask?" Elizabeth hedged. She didn't want to tell Todd that Courtney's smile was stuck in her mind like a bad dream. Even if Mr. Thomas's alluring daughter *did* have her eye on Todd, to think that he returned her feelings—well, that was simply a result of her writer's imagination gone haywire. Todd was only being friendly, as he'd explained already.

"You're awfully quiet tonight," Todd persisted.

Elizabeth shrugged. "Just digesting that big dinner, I guess." It was at least part of the truth.

"It was great, wasn't it?" Todd patted his stomach. "Except when your sister decided to start in on Courtney." His brow wrinkled in a little frown, visible in the glowing light of a full moon.

"I don't know what you're talking about, Todd." A flicker of annoyance danced in the depths of Elizabeth's blue-green eyes. Todd's less-than-enthusiastic feelings toward her twin were the one consistent sore spot in their relationship. "If anything, Courtney was at fault, acting like a prima donna at the mention of canned stew. With an attitude like that, I don't see how she's going to make it to day two of the trip."

"And with an attitude like yours, she's not going to have much help, is she? Besides, you know that Jessica was just waiting to pounce on Courtney."

"You think so?" There were icicles in Elizabeth's voice.

Todd stopped walking and faced Elizabeth. "Aw, Liz, I didn't mean to get you so upset." His tone was apologetic. "Look, I'm sorry if I said anything about Jessica that offended you. Really I am."

Elizabeth stared straight ahead, past Todd, into the moonlit night. Why couldn't he see that there was more than just Jessica on her mind?

"Liz, what is it?" Todd leaned forward and took one of her hands in his.

She offered no resistance but didn't reach out to meet him halfway, either. "I guess it's nothing," she answered finally. At least she hoped with all her might that it was nothing. All the same, as Elizabeth was falling asleep that night, Courtney's face flashed in her mind, and her stomach did a slow, uneasy somersault.

Four

"Whew!" Jessica exclaimed, wiping her forehead with the back of her hand as she got off her bicycle. "I'd like to see about turning this thing in for a motorized model. These mountains are really doing me in,"

"Truer words were never spoken," Lila agreed, leaning her sleek bike against a giant pine tree. "What I want to know is: when do we get to the downhill part of the ride?" The road out of Los Angeles that morning had climbed almost steadily into the mountains.

Jessica plopped herself down on the ground, soft with a blanket of pine needles, and squinted up at her friend, "Didn't they tell you, Lila? There *is* no downhill on this trip. You just keep going up and up." She whistled a few bars of the theme music from "The Twilight Zone."

Lila lay back on the earth next to Jessica, her

light-brown hair spread out around her head. "If that's true, I quit right this instant!"

"Before lunch?" asked Jessica. "God. I'm so ravenous, I could eat a horse."

"You may have to," Lila quipped. "Judging from the kind of meals we've been having on the road so far."

"Naw," Jessica assured her. "It's Annie's turn to make lunch. Trust little Miss Diligence to come up with something perfect."

In a clearing several yards away, Annie Whitman sat at a picnic table, slicing vegetables. Ms. Dalton and Roger Patman were building a campfire nearby. The others sat around nursing sore muscles or writing postcards.

"Besides," Jessica said, giving Lila a swat on the arm, "if you keep making comments about the food, people are going to start mixing you up with little Miss You-Know-Who."

Lila rolled over to face Jessica. "Don't even joke about that," she said fiercely. "That girl is going to drive me right up the wall. 'Bruce, how do these bags attach to my bike? Oh, can you do it for me? Todd, will you be a dear and massage my back? It aches s-o-o-o much from riding,' " Lila mimicked. "Yecch."

Jessica nodded. "All with that brand-new and very suspicious act." Her lip curled up in a sneer of disgust.

"Are you two positive you're not just a teensy

bit jealous of all the attention Courtney's getting?" a girl's voice asked.

Jessica whirled around to see Olivia on the other side of the pine tree, reaching into one of her saddlebags for her mess kit. "Well, well, it looks like we've got a visitor." She fixed Olivia with an icy stare. "For your information, Liv, I wouldn't trade places with Courtney for all the money in her father's bank account."

"Me, neither," Lila chimed in, sitting up. "With her Little Miss Sunshine act, there's still one thing she can't hide—that she's totally helpless. I mean, she's so used to being waited on hand and foot, she can't do anything for herself."

Jessica fought the urge to snicker. Of all people, Lila was hardly the one to talk about being waited on hand and foot. Back at Fowler Crest, Lila lived like a queen. She could have been describing herself just as easily as Courtney Thomas.

Still, Lila was right about Courtney. "Yeah, she may act tough, riding around with that skinhead boyfriend of hers, but when you come right down to it, she's just too delicate for this trip."

She glanced over at Courtney, who watched like a perfect student as Todd knelt by her bicycle, adjusting the front brake.

"And what a slowpoke," Lila added. "She's almost as bad as Barry."

"Speaking of which, where is the boy wonder anyway? Still struggling back near L.A., somewhere?" Jessica burst out laughing at her own joke, and Lila joined her.

Olivia didn't appear to be at all amused. "Actually," she said, "I think he went to that general store we passed a few miles back. Annie forgot to buy drinks for lunch, so Barry volunteered to go get some. Liz went with him."

Jessica sighed. "Trust my softhearted sister to get stuck helping that wimp all the time. When is she going to take my advice and wise up a little?"

"Well, you know, Jess," Lila responded slyly, "I'm sure Barry wouldn't have minded in the least if you had gone along with him instead of Liz."

Jessica shot Lila a look of pure venom. "Do you have to remind me? Every time I turn around, there's that tub of lard, just standing there staring at me. Although I must say"— Jessica's tone grew rich with amusement— "Butterball does have great taste!" She put her hand behind her blond head and struck a hilarious cover-girl pose.

Even Olivia laughed that time. "Can we quote you on that, Jess?"

Jessica quickly snapped to attention. "No! Absolutely not!" She snapped. "I don't want that jelly-belly getting the idea that I approve of his little crush." She turned up her nose in disgust. "No. I prefer to keep him as far from me as

49

possible. And if that means Liz's getting saddled with him, well—better her than me." Jessica brushed some pine needles off her shorts. "Although I'm sure Liz is helping him out this time just so she doesn't have to look at Courtney and Todd together." She shook her head fiercely. "Why does Liz put up with that? I always told her Todd was no good."

"Come on, Jessica," interjected Olivia. "Todd's the nicest guy in the world. He's only trying to make things easier for Courtney. You heard what she told us. She really didn't want to come on this trip at all. And even though she's trying to be a good sport about it, I think she's pretty unhappy about the whole thing. Todd just wants to make her feel better."

"Yeah, maybe, but he's making Liz feel worse." Indignation colored Jessica's words. "No one has the right to do that to my sister! And anyway, the oh-so-beautiful Courtney Thomas doesn't have a single reason to feel sorry for herself. This trip is a vacation, not a jail sentence."

"Look, maybe with a little time Courtney will come around to our way of thinking about it," Olivia said. "She's already made one pretty spectacular self-improvement. I don't think a second one is entirely out of the question."

"Well, as for the first self-improvement, as you put it, I'd bet my dinner duty for the next two weeks that it's nothing but a big act. Any day

now, Courtney's fangs are going to start showing again," Jessica declared. "Just you wait and
see."

"I'm not the betting type," Olivia replied,
closing up her saddlebag and heading back
toward the picnic table. "But it would be nice if
you two could pull in your own fangs a little and
give Courtney a chance," she concluded over her
shoulder.

Lila made a grimace at Olivia's receding back.
"She's going to pay for that," she muttered.

Jessica shrugged. "Lila, what do you care what
Olivia thinks, anyway. If I were you, I'd save my
energy. We've got more important things to take
care of." A wicked gleam came into Jessica's
aqua eyes as she glanced over in Courtney's
direction.

"OK, Wakefield. Spill it!" Lila said eagerly.

"Well, the goal is to get Courtney off the trip,
right?"

Lila nodded.

"Because with her out of the way, Todd won't
be making Liz feel so rotten. And more impor-
tantly, we'll get her out of our own hair."

"What do you have in mind, Jess?" Lila's
brown eyes gleamed conspiratorially.

"Well, according to Courtney, her father is
sending her on this trip for her own benefit—to
toughen her up. But I can't believe he'd want her
to be miserable. I mean, I think he figures she'll
start enjoying herself if she makes friends with

51

people who don't have a thing for spiked hair and chains."

"You mean, people like us," Lila said.

"Exactly. But when he finds out that the nice boys and girls he wants his darling daughter to be with are doing a number on her, he's going to let her come home in a flash. After all, he wanted this trip to be for precious Courtney's good. When he finds out she's unhappy, well . . . I think the outcome is guaranteed.

"What's more, Courtney herself said it wasn't her decision to come on this trip. In the long run, we'll be doing her a big favor. We don't even have to feel the slightest bit guilty about it. Meanwhile, I wouldn't mind making her squirm a little." A satisfied grin slowly spread across Jessica's face.

Lila nodded slowly. "Well, then, what's the plan?"

"We'll have to wait until our next camping stop. But something cold and clammy in the bottom of her sleeping bag might be a good start."

"Sounds great!" Lila said enthusiastically. "And, Jess, if it works on Courtney, maybe we can start using the same approach on Ms. Dalton."

Jessica gave her friend a tiny frown. "Lila, why are you always so down on her? She gave me an A last semester." As the topic moved from Courtney to Ms. Dalton, Jessica became fairness itself, changing her tone as easily as a fashion model changes clothes. "And she's having a hard enough time with Mr. Collins. She doesn't need you to make it any worse. Have you noticed that those two have barely spoken a word to each other since we left Sweet Valley?"

Lila nodded. "Not that I blame Mr. Collins."

"Come on, Lila," Jessica said. "She's not so bad."

"That's because you don't know her like I do." Lila swiveled around and watched the slender, dark-haired woman coaxing life into the camp fire. "If she were around *your* house all the time, sponging off *your* father. . . ." Her mouth twisted into an ugly scowl as her voice trailed off.

"Lila, you're not going to see your father for the rest of the month—and neither will Ms. Dalton." Jessica chose her words carefully. "So maybe now's a chance for you to stop vying for his attention and start learning what Ms. Dalton is really like."

Lila's scowl turned to a look of total astonishment. "Jess, if I didn't know any better, I'd swear that was Elizabeth talking!"

Suddenly a deep red stained Jessica's cheeks. "Maybe the group spirit of this trip has gotten to me a little," she said uncomfortably. "But that doesn't mean I'm going to be soft on Courtney," she added quickly, saving face and returning to the original subject in one deft move. "Not a chance."

*   *   *

Elizabeth squeezed her eyes shut to block out the image of Todd and Courtney laughing and talking over lunch as if they were the best of friends. When she opened them again, Charlie Markus was in front of her, helping himself to the last bite of dessert.

"Boy, that meal was delicious!" he said, popping a chocolate-covered strawberry in his mouth and licking his fingers. "Annie, where'd you learn to cook like that?" he called over to her.

Annie's cheeks turned pink, and she seemed flustered that the compliment had come from Charlie. "Oh, it's no big deal," she mumbled, looking at the ground.

She had prepared a hearty cheese fondue and mixed salad, followed by a luscious chocolate fondue with pieces of banana, apple, and strawberries, all from ingredients she'd found in a tiny roadside grocery store.

Bruce watched Annie and Charlie's exchange with his upper lip curled in disapproval. "It's only one of her many hidden talents," he said snidely to his friend. "Of course, she has one talent that every guy in Sweet Valley knows about." His comment was just loud enough for everyone to overhear.

Elizabeth clenched her fists. How dare Bruce Patman! Everyone knew that Annie had become a completely different person since the beginning of the year. Her days of seeking attention in the arms of any boy who came along were a thing of the past. Annie had long since learned that one faithful companion was better than a whole roomful of fickle ones.

Now Annie blushed again, but this time out of shame and humiliation. She lowered her beautiful face, and Elizabeth could see a tear glistening in the corner of one of her big brown eyes.

Charlie looked at Annie, then at Bruce, then back at Annie, and at Bruce again. It was plain to Elizabeth that he was uncomfortably caught between Annie and his tennis team buddy.

Finally Charlie just shook his head, a lock of thick, dark hair falling over his forehead, and walked over to his bicycle. He removed his water bottle from its holder and feigned great concentration as he poured a bit of the liquid onto his dirty plate, wiped it off, then rinsed it, being careful to save some of the water for the next leg of the trip.

Annie followed his cue and began preparing her own equipment for the afternoon ride.

Soon the unpleasant incident was behind them, though hardly forgotten, Elizabeth supposed. She herself had trouble putting the memory of it aside. She adjusted her bike helmet and joined the others as they got back on the road.

Switching gears on her bicycle for the long incline in front of her, Elizabeth suddenly had a flash of understanding. So that was why Annie had been acting so coldly toward Charlie! She'd probably assumed that Bruce was telling him stories about her and that consequently Charlie was after only one thing from her.

Perhaps the scene Elizabeth had just witnessed hadn't been the first one. Bruce Patman was capable of making trouble when he put his mind to it. And Charlie? He seemed to be a nice enough guy. Nevertheless, he was Bruce's friend, so who could say for sure where he really stood in all of this?

Poor Annie. She was as sweet and good as she was lovely to look at, with her slender legs, her curly dark hair, and her perfect, even features. She deserved better than the nasty reminders of her former life that Bruce Patman was doling out to her.

It was a shame that Bruce couldn't forget about the past. And also a shame that amidst these other problems, Elizabeth was troubled by something as unimportant as Courtney's tinkly laugh.

A couple of hours later, she was still brooding as Roger and Olivia, at the front of the pack, steered their bicycles over to the side of the road. They were followed immediately afterward by Bruce and then, one by one, the rest of the group.

Elizabeth got off her bicycle, stretched her lean, sun-bronzed legs, and admired the vista from the summit of the mountains. The view of the shimmering Pacific Ocean far below was breathtaking, yet Elizabeth couldn't help thinking things could be a lot better.

As she stood there, Todd came over and put his arm around her shoulder in a gesture that should have been a comfort to her. "Pretty, huh?" he commented.

She nodded but remained distant.

"Hey, you don't mind if I share the view with you, do you?" He planted a soft kiss on her cheek.

"Of course I don't mind," Elizabeth made herself say. "Why should I?" She tried to keep her tone light, but her voice sounded strange to her ears—tight and tense.

"Liz, you're not mad at me about something, are you?" Todd asked.

"Mad?" Elizabeth shook her head. "No, in fact, it's nice to have a few minutes alone with you." Suddenly as she spoke, she became aware of the truth of her own words. "I know you've been riding right along with me and the rest of the group all day, but somehow—somehow I feel as if I haven't had a chance to be with you."

"Yeah, well, Courtney has needed a lot of help with her bicycle and stuff," Todd responded offhandedly. He glanced over at Courtney, who was just pulling off the road.

Elizabeth stiffened again.

"Hey, you're not mad about my giving her a few pointers on her first day of riding, are you?"

Todd looked Elizabeth straight in the eye. "Because you know that when it comes right down to it, there's only one girl on this trip for me. And I'm holding her in my arms right this instant."

Elizabeth studied her boyfriend's handsome face, his strong jaw, his coffee-brown eyes, and the shock of wavy hair that often fell across his brow. "Are you sure?" she asked.

"Oh, Liz, of course I am. No one else could ever be as special to me as you are."

"No one?" Elizabeth looked pointedly in Courtney's direction.

"Liz, let's get something straight. I want Courtney to know she can count on me for help and for friendship. And I hope she'll be able to count on your friendship, too. But it ends there."

Elizabeth still felt a twinge of doubt. "If it were any other way, wouldn't you be afraid to tell me?" she asked in a small voice.

"But it isn't any other way! Liz, you're the most important person in the world to me. I wish you'd believe that," Todd implored.

Elizabeth finally felt the last remnants of uncertainty over Todd ebbing away. Her shoulders relaxed, and she breathed a sigh of relief.

Todd drew her tightly against his chest and held her with his strong arms. "Now, how about a smile?" He pulled back just enough to see her face.

But as he did, Elizabeth caught a glimpse of

Annie, sitting apart from the other kids and staring forlornly into the distance. Despite Todd's loving arms around her, Elizabeth felt unhappy.

"Hey, Liz," Todd gave her a slight shake. "Now what is it?"

"Oh, Todd," she said, resting her head on his chest, "it's so beautiful here. I know I should just be happy."

Todd wrinkled his forehead. "There's a 'but' in there, somewhere, though."

Elizabeth swallowed hard and nodded. She was on the verge of telling him about Annie when Bruce's all-too-familiar voice carried through the air.

"Well, well, if it isn't Bionic Barry, zooming up the hill with the strength of twenty men!" Elizabeth and Todd turned to see Barry Cooper approaching, huffing and puffing, his face bright red as he pushed his bicycle up the last part of the incline. Behind him rode Mr. Collins, whose turn it was to bring up the rear of the procession.

Jessica and Lila cracked up at Bruce's joke. Some of the other kids giggled too. "Bionic Barry! Oh, that's great," Lila said, "I hate to give you credit, Bruce, but that name fits the little nerd perfectly."

Roger spoke up in Barry's defense. "Hey, Bruce, why don't you leave the guy alone? He's trying as hard as he can, and I haven't heard him complain at all. Unlike some of you."

"You tell him, Roger," Elizabeth said softly.

But Roger didn't have the last say.

"My cousin." Bruce pronounced the word "cousin" as if it were the kiss of death. "Yes, I should have known you would stick up for the underdog. After all, *you* were an underdog for most of your life, weren't you?"

Elizabeth could see Roger gritting his teeth. There was a moment of tense silence.

Then, to everyone's surprise, Charlie stepped forward and put a hand on Bruce's shoulder. "Don't you think you've put down enough people today?" he asked his friend quietly.

Bruce was clearly startled. It was one thing to be at odds with Annie or Barry or Roger. But Charlie was his friend. Charlie was supposed to be on his side. Bruce's face reddened, and he didn't say another word for the entire rest stop.

As the group was getting back on their bicycles for the last ten miles of the day, Elizabeth saw Charlie go over to Annie and talk to her in a low voice. He had obviously thought about the lunchtime scene as much as Elizabeth had, and now he was making amends.

Elizabeth smiled—the first real smile since they'd left Los Angeles. Maybe Charlie was a friend of the unscrupulous Bruce Patman, but he was turning out to be an OK guy.

"Now that's what I like to see," said Todd, drinking in his girlfriend's happy expression. He kissed the top of her head. "Just remember that I love you," he said. Then he threw his leg over his bicycle and started back on the road.

Courtney managed to be right behind him, but this time Elizabeth found honestly that it didn't bother her. Things were right with her and Todd again, and Annie's lovely smile was back on her face.

While she headed for the long awaited downhill section of the day's ride, Elizabeth hummed quietly to herself. It looked as if it might just turn out to be a great trip after all.

Five

"Yippee! Home sweet home," yelled Jessica, pulling into the driveway of the large, wooden building the youth hostel occupied. "At least for tonight!"

Around her, the gently swaying trees were silhouetted against the sky as the sun began its descent. Jessica could hear the waves breaking against the shore just behind the dunes that surrounded the hostel. She breathed deeply and smelled the ocean. "Mmm, this is the life," she said to Lila, unfastening her saddlebags from her bike. "I mean, when the cycling's over for the day!"

Lila nodded in agreement.

The two girls locked their bicycles up, took their bags and other equipment, and headed inside the spacious house. The houseparents, a thin bearded man in his late twenties and a woman of about the same age with long blond hair, were already welcoming some of the other kids and stamping their hostel passes.

"Hi, I'm Dave," the young man said as he stamped Jessica's pass with a miniature seascape in purple ink. "And this is my wife, Joanna."

But his words were lost on Jessica. Her attention had been caught by a suntanned boy with chestnut-colored curls, coming down the staircase at the far end of the hostel. He was wearing a pair of well-worn jeans and a tight black T-shirt that revealed his muscular arms.

Jessica inhaled sharply. This guy was too gorgeous for words! She quickly ran her fingers through her hair and tucked her tank top into her cut-off shorts to make herself look more presentable. But before she had a chance to catch the boy's eye, he was out the door, followed by another boy—a stockier, darker-haired version of himself.

"Omigod. Did you get a look at that guy?" Jessica whispered out of the corner of her mouth, poking Lila in the ribs.

"Which one?" Lila hissed back. "They're all over the place!" She nodded to a room off the entranceway, where several kids were playing cards, reading, writing postcards, or sitting around, talking.

"That's the common room," said the housemother, Joanna, following Lila and Jessica's gaze. "And now that your whole group is here, we can show you the rest of the house."

As they passed the common room, Lila gave a little wave in the direction of the three card players—a lanky, dark-skinned boy, another boy with a blue bandanna fastened around his neck, and their sandy-haired companion. Jessica flashed them her most irresistible smile. The boys grinned and waved back.

"Engaging in your favorite sport?" came a snide voice in back of Jessica.

"Oh, can it, Bruce. You're not so pure and innocent yourself," Jessica chided him. "You like to girl-watch every bit as much as we like to boy-watch," she continued. "Take that blonde over by the window, for instance."

Bruce looked at the girl Jessica had referred to. "Umm. For once you're right, Jessica. I think I will take her. . . ."

"There's something for everyone, here," Jessica commented to Lila as they entered the hostel kitchen. "Even the oh-so-choosy Bruce Patman."

Bruce and Jessica's ongoing feud dated back to the stormy end of their brief but much-talked-about romance, early in the school year. Though they'd finally reached a state of uneasy peace, there were always moments when the old verbal battle surfaced.

"And an almost unbearable number of possibilities for the not-so-choosy Jessica Wakefield," Bruce shot back.

"Bruce, there was only one rotten choice I ever

made." Jessica stuck her tongue out at him. Besides, she thought to herself, Bruce couldn't possibly be further from the truth. Sure, there were lots of good-looking guys around to practice her smile on, but Jessica had her mind on one and only one. That single glimpse of him on the staircase had been enough to make her certain. The curly-haired boy was the one for Jessica.

As she conjured up images of the two of them walking on the beach under a perfect, star-speckled sky, Dave and Joanna droned on about hostel procedures.

"Here's the sign-up list for kitchen time," Joanna was saying. She pointed toward a sheet of paper next to the stove. "This way we don't end up with ten different people trying to cook dinner in here at the same time."

"Lila, Courtney," said Mr. Collins. "Since you two are on cooking duty tonight, it'll be your responsibility to sign up for time, OK?"

Lila made no effort to stifle a groan. "Of all the people to get stuck with," she complained to Jessica.

Courtney nodded dutifully like the good little angel she'd become, but not before Jessica noticed the scowl that had momentarily appeared on her face. *The old Courtney*, thought Jessica, *boiling right under the surface of her super-sweet frosting.*

But the moment slipped away in a flash, and

Courtney's halo was back on her head again. Still, that didn't change the fact that she had probably never so much as boiled a kettle of water in her privileged life. And, actually, now that Jessica thought about it, Lila probably hadn't either.

As they left the kitchen, Lila cast a backward glance at the stove, eyeing it suspiciously as if it were some kind of never-before-encountered monster from outer space.

"Maybe we ought to go out for dinner tonight," Jessica whispered to her twin as the group was led upstairs to the dorm rooms.

"That's not the worst idea you've had all day," Elizabeth whispered back, as the twins followed Joanna toward the girls' dorm, the boys and Mr. Collins going in another direction with Dave.

As she stepped through the door, Jessica found herself in a huge room, filled with metal-frame bunk beds like the ones she remembered from her summer at sleep-away camp. Staking her claim, she quickly put her things on an unoccupied upper bed next to a window with a great view of the mountains in the distance.

"Curfew is eleven o'clock and wake-up time is seven-thirty," Joanna said to a chorus of moans and grumbles. "And we ask that you be out by nine. Otherwise, you're required to pay a day fee." The young housemother explained a few other rules and regulations and then left the group to themselves.

No more than five minutes later, Jessica and Lila were back downstairs in the common room, trading stories with the card players, who had been joined by two of the girls from their trip.

Lila's eagerness to make friends was as obvious as a connect-the-dots drawing. Within no time, she was flirting madly with Tom, the one Jessica thought of as "the bandanna boy." "You mean, your group has cycled all the way from Colorado?" Lila was saying, her brown eyes wide with awe.

Jessica's motives were not quite as transparent. While her friend drowned Tom with charm, Jessica carefully moved the topic of discussion toward the other kids at the hostel, manipulating the conversation like a seasoned politician. "I'll bet you meet some pretty interesting people at these places," she said. "Like right under this very roof for example." Silently she pictured the curly-haired boy.

"Oh, definitely," one of the girls said. Sally, Jessica thought her name was. "You see that guy over there?" Sally pointed to a well-built, black-haired boy playing checkers with the blond girl Jessica had pointed out to Bruce earlier.

Jessica nodded.

"Well, he wants to be an Olympic bike racer. Every day he covers more ground than we cover in a week."

"Really?" Jessica feigned interest, coaxing Sally to talk about various other kids staying at the hostel. Finally, she made her move. "And what about the guy with lightish, curly hair, probably about six feet or so? And another guy who looks a little like him, but shorter and darker. I saw them as we were coming in."

"Oh, you mean Robbie and Danny October," said the boy who had introduced himself as Stewart. "They're brothers. Robbie's the taller one."

"Yeah, the two of them are traveling on their own," Sally put in. "Totally wild. They're probably out looking for action this minute."

"Sounds like they've got the right idea," Jessica commented. *And it sounds like this Robbie is my kind of guy*, she added to herself.

"I don't know," said the other girl, a petite redhead with a face full of freckles. "They're always getting into trouble. I heard that they got kicked out of the first hostel they were in for throwing beer bottles out the window."

"Yeah, and last night they came back after curfew and had to climb through a window to get in," Stewart said.

But rather than discourage Jessica, the stories about Robbie and his brother only intrigued her.

"Unfortunately for you," the redhead continued, "you may be seeing a lot of those guys. They're cycling north along the coast, just like you. I wouldn't be surprised if you cross paths again."

Jessica allowed herself a tiny, self-satisfied

grin. Her work was done for now. She'd found out all she needed to know. Robbie and his brother were riding the same route that she was! Well, that made it simple. The gorgeous chestnut-haired boy was as good as hers!

Dearest Nolan,

I'm holding my breath until I see you again.

My plan is off to a good start, so it shouldn't be much more than a week, but even that is too long.

I don't know how anyone can call this a vacation. It's more like boot camp—work, work, work to get my bicycle up and down these hills all day, and then, when we get to where we're going, more work—shopping and cooking and cleaning chores around this two-bit joke of a hotel they call a youth hostel. In a half hour, for instance, I'll be cooking dinner for all these perfect little boy scouts and girl scouts who are supposed to be my new friends. And all with a sickeningly sweet smile on my face. It's enough to make a person scream!

But it's worth it, if it means I'll be seeing you soon. And there's no reason why I shouldn't be. Already, most of the little dears are warming up to me. And one in particular is going to make my whole plan possible.

His name is Todd, and he's just the kind of boy you can bring home to meet Daddy. Which is exactly what I intend to be doing very soon. Daddy thought Todd was a "perfect gentleman," and when he hears about Todd and me, he's sure to forget all his worries over "that horrible Nolan Ruggers" (Oh, darling, I miss you so much) and let me come right home. With Todd by my side, of course. But not to worry. We'll think of some good way to keep him out of our hair.

The only hitch so far, is Todd's girlfriend, Elizabeth, a shoo-in for Miss Teenage America, if ever I saw one. You know the type—blond and blue-eyed with a baby-doll smile, honor-roll student, writes for the school newspaper. Any second you expect to see her helping some old lady across the street.

Courtney glanced across the backyard of the hostel to where Elizabeth sat reading under a tree, Todd by her side. Elizabeth looked up, as if feeling Courtney's eyes on her, and gave a weak smile.

Elizabeth and Todd are a matched set of do-gooders, so getting between the two of them could prove a little tricky. Not to worry, though. I'm not easily defeated. First, Mr. Sympathy is going to be defenseless against the carefully made-up stories I intend to start telling him—my deepest confidences about Daddy, my home life, the secret "real" reason for this trip—the fictional works. And second, even without the stories, I already detect a note of tension between the precious lovebirds, and you can bet that it's on my account. Elizabeth's trying her best to be nice to me, but I can tell that she doesn't trust me. Which is just as it should be. Because when Todd realizes how unfeeling she is toward me, he's going to start wondering if she really is Miss Perfect, after all. That's when I move in for the kill.

I have to admit that this business with Elizabeth is the most interesting part of the trip—something to occupy my mind during all those dreadful hours of bicycle riding, and even more dreadful hours with my tripmates. Nolan, if only you were here, things would get interesting in a hurry. But since it's not to be, I'll just concentrate on getting home as quickly as possible. It shouldn't be hard, thanks to Todd and Elizabeth.

Well, kitchen duty calls (Can you believe it? *Me* making dinner?), so I have to sign off now. Party extra hard for both of us.

Kisses and more,
Courtney

"Better late than never!" Todd joked as the

group finally sat down for dinner several hours later than they'd planned.

"And better pizza than that burned, gooey mess we almost had to eat," Bruce said, sounding almost happy that someone else had ruined a meal, too. "Thank goodness for the pizza place!"

Lila had insisted that she'd watched her housekeeper prepare fried chicken enough times to be able to master it herself, but after a certifiable kitchen disaster, she and Courtney had ended up dipping into their almost inexhaustible trip allowances for several take-out pizzas.

"Although it was worth the time in the kitchen," Lila whispered to Jessica. "Because I managed to stick Courtney with the job of coating the chicken. Ugh! Boy, you should have seen her. I thought she was going to have a fit!"

"Uh-huh," Jessica answered, only half listening to her friend as she kept her eyes fastened on the door to the entranceway for gorgeous Robbie October.

"Jess, are you listening?" Lila bit into a slice of pepperoni pizza. "I swear I saw the old Courtney for a minute when I told her what she had to do in the kitchen. I think we're starting to get to her."

"What? Oh, yeah, great," replied Jessica. "Hey, do you think Robbie and his brother are ever going to get back?"

"Oh, so that's where your mind is." Lila rolled her eyes. "I should have guessed. Actually, Jess, my bet is that they're going to sneak in after curfew, just like they did last night. If I were you, I wouldn't plan on spending any time with him this evening."

"Well, you're not me," Jessica snapped. "Besides, you're just sour about wasting all your time cooking, when you could have been going after the bandanna boy. And if you can't have fun, you don't want me to, either."

"For your information, Jessica, Tom and I are going out for a walk right after we're finished with dinner." Lila reached for another slice of pizza.

"Oh," Jessica said sullenly. The evening was not working out the way she'd planned. Lila was getting all the breaks, and she wasn't getting any.

"Cheer up, Jess. You'll probably get to see Robbie again somewhere farther up the coast. And even if you don't, there'll be tons of other guys."

"Maybe." But Jessica continued to feel sorry for herself. She picked at her pizza and barely touched her dessert—a rich chocolate cake, also purchased with Lila and Courtney's "pocket money."

After dinner, Jessica moped around the common room, getting up and peering out toward the front door every few minutes.

There was still no sign of Robbie by the time lights-out approached. Jessica stayed downstairs right up until the last possible moment, when Joanna appeared to lock up.

"Elizabeth, isn't it?" she said warmly.

"Jessica. Liz is my sister."

"Oh, yes. The twins. Well, Jessica, I'm afraid it's that time of night."

Jessica glared at Joanna as if the whole miserable evening of waiting in vain had been her fault.

"Bedtime," Joanna clarified gently.

Jessica clicked her tongue against the roof of her mouth in annoyance and exasperation as she rose from the common-room sofa. Finally she dragged herself upstairs.

To make matters worse, when Jessica got up to the dorm room, Courtney was already the center of attention.

"Oh, what fun!" she was exclaiming to Sally, who had the bunk under hers. "It's just like being at a slumber party!"

"Or having a big family!" Annie Whitman chimed in.

"I always wondered what that would be like," said Sally.

"Me, too," agreed Courtney, everybody's new friend. "It gets awfully lonely in that big house sometimes."

Jessica made her way over to the other side of the large room. "Listen to her. Somebody ought to get out a violin," she muttered to Lila, who was sitting starry-eyed on the edge of her bed after her walk with Tom. "Like she really had it that bad, growing up with all that loot."

Elizabeth, in the next bunk over, propped herself up on her elbow. "You know, Jess, I've been thinking. Maybe we're being too rough on her."

Jessica stared at her twin as if she'd sprouted another head. "Too tough? On *her*? Liz, what kind of nonsense has that boyfriend of yours been pumping into your head?"

"What makes you think Todd has anything to do with this?" Elizabeth asked. Jessica could hear her sister struggling to keep the defensive note out of her voice.

"Liz, you don't have to look too hard to see that Todd has become Courtney's great defender, along with some others on our trip, who are fooled just as easily." Jessica eyed Annie and Olivia as they chatted with Courtney.

"Jessica, it just so happens that Todd loves me, not Courtney," Elizabeth said. "He even told me so this afternoon."

Jessica shrugged. "She's still managing to get more time with him than you have recently." Jessica could tell by the look on her sister's face that she had hit home. She wasn't trying to hurt Elizabeth, but she wanted to make sure her twin knew the score. Nothing could be so humiliating as turning your boyfriend over to another girl without a fight.

Of course, in Jessica's book, Todd wasn't worth a whole lot—he was always around taking up too much of Elizabeth's time—but she wasn't going to sit around and watch Courtney win an easy victory over her twin.

"Don't you worry about anything, though, Liz," she said. "Lila and I are going to take care of dear old Courtney, aren't we, Lila?" She winked significantly at her friend.

"Mm. Uh-huh," mumbled Lila, stretched out on her bed now, lost in memories of her evening on the beach.

Elizabeth fixed her blue-green eyes on Jessica. "OK. What are you two demons cooking up this time?"

"Don't trouble yourself about the details, Liz," Jessica whispered. "Just leave us experts to worry about the plan."

Or rather, "plans," she added to herself. *Because I have a plan for Robbie October, too.* Her thoughts left Courtney and returned to the boy who had been on her mind all night. Maybe he'd slipped away from her this time, but it wouldn't happen again. The next time Robbie appeared on the scene, she intended to make absolutely sure he noticed her. And she didn't plan to stop there. . . .

Six

"ABC, it's easy as one, two, three . . ." The song blared from the jukebox in the campground canteen as Elizabeth and Todd danced energetically, turning and jumping to the beat of an old Jackson Five song. Next to them, Jessica whirled around with Mr. Collins, while some of the other kids downed ice-cold Cokes and tapped their feet to the beat.

"Feels great to have my feet on the ground," Elizabeth shouted to Todd above the music.

"I know what you mean," Todd yelled back. "I think my legs are starting to make bicycle motions in my sleep."

"Well, only one more day of hard riding before the Santa Barbara stopover," Elizabeth reminded him. She was referring to the three days the group was to spend at a beautiful campground near a crystal-clear glacial pond. The stop had become the subject of much conversation because it would be the first time since Los Angeles that the group could forget about their bicycles for more than an evening.

"Ah, yes. Santa Barbara. Haven for weary travelers," Todd joked, clapping his hands as a new song came on the jukebox.

Elizabeth moved to the music and watched out of the corner of her eye as Charlie held a hand out to Annie and motioned toward the dancers. To Elizabeth's delight, Annie took his hand in hers.

But as the two of them were moving onto the floor, Courtney, too, was making her way toward the dancers. More specifically, she was heading straight for Todd.

Elizabeth couldn't blame Todd for standing transfixed as Courtney sashayed up to him and swirled her long, silky scarf around his arm, then pulled him toward her. She might not have been much on a bicycle or in a kitchen, but when it came to dancing, Courtney had had plenty of practice, in the most chic clubs in the world.

Todd looked over at Elizabeth, shrugged his shoulders, and grinned sheepishly.

Elizabeth forced herself to smile back. She had promised herself that she wouldn't let Courtney get the better of her, and she had every intention of keeping that promise. All the same, she moved off the floor, leaving Todd and Courtney to dance by themselves. Because where Courtney was concerned, three was definitely a crowd.

On the other side of the room, Barry Cooper was trying a far less insistent method of getting a dance partner than Courtney had. He shyly shuffled over to Jessica, who had just gotten off the dance floor, and mumbled what Elizabeth imagined to be a few flustered, barely intelligible words.

As she bought herself a root beer and carried it to a table in the corner of the room, Elizabeth could hear her sister's laugh of scorn. Barry quickly walked away, his head down, his ears bright red.

Elizabeth frowned her disapproval in her twin's direction, but the gesture was wasted. Jessica was too busy whispering something in Lila's ear. Lila kept nodding, the corners of her mouth turning up in a sly grin.

What were the two angels up to now? Elizabeth wondered. A plot to humiliate poor Barry Cooper further? In that department, Elizabeth thought he did well enough on his own.

Elizabeth rose from her chair, ready to stop her twin's scheme, when she saw Jessica glance at Courtney, a menacing look in her eye. Suddenly Elizabeth remembered her sister's words about "taking care of that girl." She sat back down abruptly. No, it wasn't Barry who was the unfortunate target of Jessica's energies after all.

Elizabeth stayed put, sipping her root beer as Jessica and Lila crept stealthily out the back door of the canteen. But as they disappeared, Elizabeth felt a teeny pinch of guilt. She had been about to stick up for Barry. Didn't Courtney deserve the same?

Every last droplet of remorse dried up in a flash, however, when Courtney let loose a silvery peal of laughter. "Oh, Todd," she gushed, "you Sweet Valley boys really know how to dance."

Elizabeth frowned, her fists clenched.

"That's because we take lessons from the Sweet Valley girls," Todd replied modestly.

The frown melted into a smile.

"Though I dare say we could all take a few lessons from you," Todd added, as Courtney executed some complicated steps for his benefit.

The smile disappeared. Courtney didn't need a single soul to stick up for her. Courtney was perfectly capable of taking care of herself.

Elizabeth drained her last few sips of soda and put her glass back down on the table with a loud thud. She had expected to be faced with steep mountain roads, long days of cycling, and the challenging adventure of wilderness living. But making sure that Courtney Thomas didn't get to her was proving to be by far the biggest test of the entire trip.

*   *   *

"Liz, can't you move over any?"

Sandwiched against the side of the green nylon tent later that night, Elizabeth felt her twin give her a swift elbow in the ribs.

"Hey, easy, Jess. If I move over any farther, I'm going to be sleeping outside."

"And don't look at me, Jessica," Lila put in. "I don't have an inch to spare."

Jessica grumbled and turned over in her sleeping bag. "They ought to make the wonderful Courtney cough up a couple hundred dollars out of her millions and spring for another tent. I mean, if it weren't for her, we'd be sleeping in twos, just like we're supposed to."

"Come on, Jess. At least we rotate. It could be worse." Elizabeth patted her twin's shoulder.

"But it could be *better*," Jessica added. "If only we could get rid of her."

"Speaking of which—" said Lila.

Suddenly a shriek pierced the fresh night air.

"Hey, that's Ms. Dalton's voice," Elizabeth noted with alarm. She wriggled out of her sleeping bag and poked her head out of the tent. Under the clear, starry sky, she could see Mr. Collins, clad only in a pair of shorts, rushing to the end of the tent Ms. Dalton was sharing with Courtney.

"Nora, are you OK?" he cried. Curiously enough, Elizabeth noticed, his voice overflowed with concern. Strange when he was barely on speaking terms with Nora Dalton.

81

But as soon as Ms. Dalton came out of her tent, looking a little shaken, but clearly all right, Mr. Collins took a few steps backward and his face froze up. "What was the noise all about?" he asked tensely.

Nora Dalton extended her hand, and with it, a small bag. Elizabeth couldn't tell what the bag contained. "This cold, horrible mess was in the bottom of my sleeping bag."

Beside her, inside the tent, Elizabeth heard her twin utter a string of curses. "Which means you blew it, Fowler," Jessica cried angrily. "How did *that* happen?"

Outside, Roger Collins was inspecting the contents of the bag. He put his nose to it, then stuck a finger inside, licked his finger, and began to laugh.

But Ms. Dalton was less amused. "I'm glad you find this so funny, Roger," she said angrily.

Mr. Collins was instantly contrite. "No, it's not that, Nora, it's just—"

"Just that you love seeing me humiliated!" Ms. Dalton's seething words rang out across the campsite.

The ugliness between the two teachers was as clear as the bright quarter moon in the sky. Elizabeth winced.

"Nora, I'm sorry," Roger Collins finally said. "I truly am. But do you know what's in this plastic bag?"

"I really didn't want to find out," Ms. Dalton replied tightly.

"It's lime Jell-O," Mr. Collins told her. "The kind you can buy at the canteen in those little paper cups."

Twitters of laughter pierced the air, coming from several different tents at once. Even Nora Dalton smiled.

"Roger, I'm sorry, too. I'm sorry I yelled at you," she said a bit formally. "Please accept my apology."

Mr. Collins nodded stiffly. Ms. Dalton held out her hand, and Mr. Collins reached toward it with his free one.

For the briefest moment, Elizabeth saw a glimmer of tenderness between the two teachers fighting to surface in a sea of tension. But the second their fingers met, they both pulled away as if they'd touched red-hot coals.

"You'll be all right?" Mr. Collins said gruffly, trying to cover up the awkward moment.

"I'm fine," Ms. Dalton returned just as uncomfortably. She turned around quickly and headed back to her tent.

"And as for all you Peeping Toms," Mr. Collins called out, his voice finally relaxing a little, "I hope you enjoyed the show."

A spontaneous round of applause and giggles came from several tents.

"For the encore, I intend to go to sleep," Mr. Collins continued. "And I suggest you do the same. We've got another full day of riding ahead of us." Then his words took on a more serious tone. "We'll discuss this incident in the morning. We all might have gotten a chuckle over the Jell-O"—he paused as laughter broke out again—"but there's simply no place for this sort of joke on this trip. If any of you feel you can't behave like a responsible, cooperative member of this group, perhaps this is not the place for you."

After that, a hush fell over the campsite, except in Elizabeth's tent. There, Jessica and Lila were still whispering heatedly.

"Look, Jess, it's not my fault. I was sure that was Courtney's sleeping bag."

"How could you make such a dumb mistake?"

"I swear, I didn't. Courtney's bag is the royal-blue one, right?"

"I don't know," Jessica said, exasperated. "That part of the plan was your job."

"Well, I did what I was supposed to do. I don't know how *that* happened." Lila made a sweeping motion in the general direction of Courtney and Ms. Dalton's tent, nearly knocking down the support pole in their own.

Elizabeth reached out to steady it.

"Lila, are you absolutely positive you didn't engineer that mix-up on purpose?" Jessica questioned pointedly. "I mean, we all know that Nora Dalton isn't your most favorite person in the world."

"Listen, Jessica. I'm telling you the truth. This

is some thanks I get for risking my neck sneaking into her tent. Next time you can do it.''

''Maybe if I had done it this time, it wouldn't have gotten so botched up.''

''Hey, you guys,'' Elizabeth said, sighing, ''hasn't there been enough excitement around here for one night? I'd like to call it a day and get some sleep.''

''I don't believe it!'' Jessica abandoned her squabble with Lila and directed her words at her sister. ''We went through all this trouble for you, and now you're trying to shut us up!''

''For me?'' Elizabeth's words reverberated in the little tent. ''Listen, Jess, from the minute you started mentioning your plans for Courtney, I didn't see how they could possibly have done anything for me.''

''Liz, I thought you were supposed to be so smart. Isn't it obvious that when Courtney's father realizes everyone's against her, he's going to let her put her bicycle on the next bus to L.A.?''

''First of all, Jess, I don't see how anyone could construe one little bag of lime Jell-O as a sign that *everyone* is against her, but that's beside the point. The real question is: What does Courtney's leaving the trip have to do with me?''

''You know, Liz, if you didn't have the good fortune to look just like me, I swear nobody would know we were sisters. It's perfectly clear that with Courtney gone, you'll have Todd's full attention again. Although I can't imagine why you think it's worth bothering with a fickle guy like that."

"Jessica Wakefield, Todd is the most loyal, caring person I know. He's only being friendly to Courtney." Elizabeth's voice was full of conviction, but inside she was less sure than she sounded. It seemed that every time she had to defend Todd against her twin, she became less and less certain of herself. True, Todd had made a special point of telling her he loved her, and she'd believed him at the time. But since then, he'd continued to cater to Courtney's every whim. Elizabeth wasn't sure how long she could go on insisting everything was fine between them.

From the other side of the tent Lila snorted, "Just being friendly, huh? Boy, I wouldn't mind a few tall, handsome 'friends' like that."

Lila's remark scored big points with Jessica, who made no effort to contain her laughter.

Elizabeth felt as if she'd had the wind knocked out of her. Tears welled up in the corners of her eyes and threatened to overflow onto her nightshirt. She tried to sniff back her sobs.

Jessica's laughter stopped abruptly. "Hey, Liz, are you crying? Liz?" Jessica put an arm around her twin's shoulder. "Liz, don't cry." Her tone was soft now, soothing. "We're only trying to help you. Really." She stroked her sister's hair to quiet her down.

Elizabeth's muffled sobs eventually subsided. She was truly touched by Jessica's concern.

Perhaps it was true that Todd had had more sensitive moments. Perhaps Jell-O in Courtney's sleeping bag wasn't the best solution. And perhaps her sister and Lila had more personal reasons for wanting Courtney off the trip. But at the very least, her twin was on her side. That much she could always count on.

Elizabeth reached over and gave Jessica a big hug. "Let's not fight anymore, OK?"

"OK," Jessica responded.

Elizabeth rolled onto her stomach and closed her eyes. "Hey, Jess," she added sleepily.

"Yeah?"

"Why lime?" Elizabeth stifled a yawn.

"Why not?" said Jessica.

It was the last thing Elizabeth remembered before falling into a deep, sound sleep. The day's events, coupled with the strenuous cycling, had been more than a match for her.

Mr. Collins called the group together the next morning at breakfast to discuss "the Jell-O incident," as it was now called.

Looking completely innocent, Jessica nursed her coffee and sat in a circle with the others.

"Perhaps it was meant as a harmless practical joke," Mr. Collins began, a frown on his strong, sun-burnished face, "but that sack of Jell-O could have broken in Ms. Dalton's sleeping bag, ruining an expensive piece of camping equipment."

Jessica shook her head solemnly as Mr. Collins continued. "Not to mention humiliating and inconveniencing her. Now I'm not going to start playing detective with you to find out who's responsible. The guilty party knows who he or she is." Mr. Collins focused on each person in turn as he spoke.

Lila lowered her head just the tiniest bit. But when the handsome teacher's eyes came to rest on Jessica, she looked right back at him, her gaze level, her expression open and honest.

"But I'm not going to tolerate another incident like this," Mr. Collins continued. "No repeat performances. Not at Ms. Dalton's expense and not at the expense of anyone else on the trip. Is that clear?"

He waited for the murmurs of "Yes, Mr. Collins." Then his grim expression melted into a warm grin. "Now, does anyone want to share this last doughnut with me?" The lecture was over.

But as Bruce and Charlie cleared up after breakfast and others took down tents and loaded their bicycles, Jessica noticed Mr. Collins at the edge of the campsite with Lila. And he didn't look happy.

Jessica watched them both gesturing angrily. She couldn't hear what was going on, but it wasn't hard to figure out. Lila had made no secret of her feelings toward Ms. Dalton. So it was no surprise that anyone would take her to be the hand behind the previous night's prank.

What was a surprise, though, was that the ever fair, levelheaded Roger Collins would lose his temper and lash out at one of the group members, especially when there was no proof that Lila was the guilty party.

A few minutes later, Lila came away clenching her fists. She headed straight for Jessica, who suddenly got very busy attaching one of the rolled-up tents to the back of her bicycle.

"That's the last time I do your dirty work," Lila stormed. "You think up the darned thing, and I get blamed for it."

Jessica continued to fiddle with the tent, averting her eyes from Lila's piercing gaze. "Look, what can I tell you? I'm sorry, but I don't know what you expected me to do."

"Well, for starters, you could have come and tried to bail me out just now."

"Lila, how was I supposed to know Mr. Collins was getting on your case? For all I knew, he could have been talking to you about the weather."

"Give me a break, Jessica. All anyone had to do to see what was going on was take one look at us. I mean the way he was chewing me out you'd think Ms. Dalton was his best friend instead of his worst enemy."

"It's interesting the way he is about her," Jessica commented, hoping to steer the subject away from Lila's heated accusations. "It's almost as if he's got two separate feelings battling inside him when it comes to that woman."

"Oh, no, you don't, Wakefield." Lila shook her head, her light-brown ponytail bobbing from side to side. "You're not getting off so easily."

Jessica reverted to defensive strategy. "You know it's really not my fault that Mr. Collins singled you out, Lila. Why blame me? Besides, how does he know you did it, anyway?"

"He said I couldn't look at him when he was talking to us."

"Well, that's true, but it's not exactly the kind of evidence that would stand up in court."

"Listen, Jess, it's your father who's the lawyer, not Mr. Collins," Lila said bitterly.

Jessica stuck out her bottom lip—the very picture of innocence wronged. "It was just my way of saying that it doesn't sound much like Mr. Collins's usual behavior. You know, justice for everyone and all that."

"You may be right about that, Jessica, but that doesn't change the fact that he did come down on *me* and that *you* weren't there to take any of the blame."

"Lila, look at it this way." Jessica played her last card, hoping to have a winning hand. "Before all this happened, Mr. Collins was probably keeping an eye on you and Ms. Dalton—I mean knowing how you feel about her. And now, he's still keeping an eye on the two of you. Nothing's really changed." It was a first-class example of Jessica Wakefield logic.

"But now, he's keeping an even closer eye on me and that—that witch. And I'm sure she thinks I did it, too."

"So?" Jessica shrugged. "You wanted to use the Courtney plan on her anyhow. And you ended up getting your way." Jessica had finally argued Lila into a corner.

"Maybe," Lila said. "But next time you've got a scheme, don't involve me in it."

"Well, OK, Lila. Then Courtney will just stay on the trip."

"What's it to me?" Lila snapped.

"For starters, you wouldn't have to look at that very sweet, very fake smile every day."

"And neither would you," Lila pointed out.

"Secondly," continued Jessica, "she wouldn't be monopolizing all the boys. I mean Todd might be the biggest sucker, but he's certainly not the only one who's falling for her tricks. And that includes the guys we've been meeting who aren't on the trip."

"I know. But that's as much a problem for you as it is for me. In fact, Jess, I hate to say it, but I'll bet that's your single biggest reason for wanting to get rid of Courtney. I know you told Elizabeth you were doing it for her, but—"

"Don't be a fool, Lila," Jessica protested. "I

couldn't care less about all those boys. There's only one on my mind now." Jessica's aqua eyes glazed over, and her voice grew soft as she pronounced Robbie October's name.

Lila rolled her eyes. "I don't doubt that Mr. October is taking up a lot of your thoughts. But somehow I'd guess that deep down you're still upset about all the attention Courtney's getting. I mean she *is* kind of stealing your place in the spotlight, isn't she?"

Jessica refused to acknowledge the truth behind her friend's words. "Lila, you make it sound like getting rid of Courtney wouldn't mean a thing to you. But if the boy problem doesn't bother you—and frankly, I don't believe that at all—I know another thing that must."

"Oh, yeah?"

"Oh, yeah. Those pearls you wear around your neck."

Lila fingered her single strand of shiny, perfect pearls. "What about them?"

"Courtney's got bigger ones. And you know that earring collection you just *had* to bring with you?"

Lila nodded slowly, a scowl darkening her face.

"I'll bet Courtney has more. And I'll bet she brought them with her, too. You *did* see those diamonds hanging from her precious pink earlobes the other night?"

Lila said nothing, and Jessica knew she had

won. "So, can I count on your help?" Jessica ran a hand through her sun-streaked, golden hair.

"I guess so," Lila said curtly.

"Good." A wide smile blossomed on Jessica's face. "I knew I could."

Seven

It was one of those magical moments that Elizabeth would remember long after she'd cycled her last mile with the group.

The group was having dinner in a hilltop restaurant, and Santa Barbara was spread out below, a vast stretch of palm trees and Spanish colonial red roofs sprinkled amidst the more modern buildings.

Everyone chattered happily, digging into the steaming hot *paella*, a seafood and rice dish that the waitress set down before them on the long balcony table.

Elizabeth turned to Todd, a satisfied smile on her face. "This restaurant is certainly worth the splurge, wouldn't you say?"

Todd nodded vigorously. "Good food, a great view, and that beautiful campsite to go back to. And you, right next to me." He leaned over and kissed Elizabeth tenderly on the cheek. "What more could anyone want?"

"Mmm. Not much," Elizabeth agreed. So far Santa Barbara had been every bit as wonderful as they had all hoped.

And in the spirit of the evening, a temporary truce seemed to be in effect for everyone on the trip.

Mr. Collins and Ms. Dalton were, if not friendly, at least civil to each other. Annie and Charlie were in their own world for two, and for once Bruce refrained from casting them the disapproving glances that made both of them so uncomfortable.

Elizabeth had no doubt that Lila and Jessica were busy thinking up a new scheme against Courtney, but for the moment, no crisis was at hand. The two girls were as content and good-spirited as everyone else. Jessica even allowed Barry the honor of sitting next to her, although she spent most of dinner talking to Lila, who was sitting on the other side of her.

And Todd was back to his usual perfect self. Elizabeth couldn't help but wonder whether it had anything to do with the fact that Courtney was not at the dinner table. But whatever the reason, it was a special treat to feel that the old Todd was back at her side.

Courtney had seemed fine all day, joking with Todd and Bruce and entertaining them all at lunchtime with a behind-the-scenes look at the big-time movie industry. Todd, an avid film buff, was particularly entranced.

But after they'd made camp and were ready to go to dinner, Courtney had said she wasn't feeling well and that they should go ahead without her. "It's just a headache," she'd explained, "but I think I'd rather lie down in my tent than get back on my bicycle."

"Well, can we bring you anything from town?" Todd was quick to ask. "Dinner, or something?"

"That's sweet of you, Todd. But I'll be OK here. There's peanut butter and fruit in the group bag, and I can probably get something else at that little store run by the campground people."

"And I have a candy bar that I didn't eat this afternoon," Annie offered. "You can have that, too."

"You're all so terrific," Courtney said. "I can't imagine what I'd do without you. But you just go ahead to dinner and have a wonderful time. Really. You don't have to worry about me." Courtney sounded so sincere, it was almost as if she had a golden halo glowing above her dark ringlets.

"Courtney, maybe someone ought to stay behind with you," Todd volunteered.

Elizabeth, in the midst of pulling a navy crewneck sweater over her head, froze. The way

Courtney had been running after Todd, she was certain to take him up on his offer.

But Courtney's response was not what Elizabeth had expected.

"No, Todd," Courtney said firmly. "You go on to dinner. Thanks, but you don't have to spoil your evening for me."

"It wouldn't be any trouble—"

"Todd, I insist." Courtney had the final word.

So there were only twelve of them on the clay-tiled balcony of the restaurant that night, watching the sun sink into the Pacific, the sky ablaze with stripes of orange and pink. Twelve of them, and a sumptuous Spanish-style banquet—the kind for which Santa Barbara was famous. Twelve of them, just as it had been before they'd ever set foot on Courtney Thomas's estate.

Elizabeth had to admit to herself that she was happier this way. And she wasn't the only member of the group who was basking in a feeling of sweet contentment.

"I think maybe I died on that last steep hill, and now I'm in bicycle heaven," Olivia joked.

"Yup," agreed Roger Patman. "All the comforts you could ever want."

"If you're not used to much," Bruce retorted, an obvious poke at his cousin's humble beginnings.

But Roger stood his ground in his own genial way. "Come on, now," he said jokingly, turning toward Bruce. "Is that any way to talk to your blood kin? Besides, I think that underneath the tough act, you're as satisfied at this minute as the rest of us."

"I think Roger may have a point there." Mr. Collins smiled his boyish smile, which had triggered so many schoolgirl crushes at Sweet Valley High.

"Yeah, 'fess up, Patman." Todd chortled.

A tiny, sheepish grin pulled at the corners of Bruce's mouth. "It isn't the worst evening I've had," he allowed.

Spontaneous applause and laughter broke out around the table.

Elizabeth raised her water glass. "I propose a toast. To Santa Barbara and more evenings when even Bruce is a happy guy."

"I'll drink to that," Bruce agreed, his chiseled features silhouetted against the dusk sky.

"And to campgrounds with beautiful lakes and hot showers!" yelled Todd.

"To *paella!*" put in Jessica.

"And good company," added Charlie, his eyes never leaving Annie's face.

"To bike trippers' paradise!" Ms. Dalton made the definitive toast.

"To bike trippers' paradise!" everyone echoed with enthusiasm.

Roger Collins was worried. True, it had been a lovely evening, but he had an unpleasant premonition that the dinner in Santa Barbara was the calm before the storm.

To begin with, Courtney Thomas had been too good to be true since they'd left Los Angeles. Mr. Collins was grateful for that, certainly, but he had a feeling that the new Courtney might vanish like a puff of smoke if—Well, he wasn't even sure what the "if" was. But in all his years of teaching high school, he had never seen a case quite like Courtney's.

Of course he'd seen kids change—lots of them, and some so completely they'd become new people. Like Annie Whitman, to pick one heartwarming example. But he'd never seen anyone change so drastically in no time at all, without any clear-cut reason for it.

Most of the kids seemed to feel that the change in Courtney was her insurance for a good trip, that if she was nice, people would be nice in return. But Roger Collins found it hard to believe that the sharp-tongued girl they'd met in Beverly Hills, the girl whose tastes ran to wild boys and insults and trouble galore, would really care what her tripmates thought of her.

Then there had been the story Courtney had concocted about why her father had sent her on this trip. Could the girl who'd been so tough and wise-talking really feel embarrassed at the true reason for her father's decision? Or was there another motive?

Roger Collins wanted to believe in the change

99

in Courtney, but there were too many unanswered questions for him to feel comfortable. So he'd continued to keep a wary eye on her.

Tonight, for instance, he wondered if she had been honest with the group. When they'd gotten back from dinner, there had been no sign of either Courtney or her bicycle. The search for her had led to the man who ran the tiny general store at the campgrounds.

Yes, a tall, dark-haired girl had been there earlier in the evening, the man said. No, she hadn't bought anything to eat. She'd wanted to use the telephone, but the telephone was broken. Oh, she'd dashed off that way, toward the bar down the road to use theirs, the man had explained.

Courtney had returned not too long afterward, full of apologies for disappearing. "I didn't realize I'd be gone so long," she'd said. "But I was feeling better, and—well, to tell the truth, I got a little lonely all by myself, so I decided to give my father a call and see how he's doing without me."

The dutiful daughter, who only days before hadn't hesitated to flaunt her disrespect for her father in front of a dozen strangers. It didn't make sense.

Roger Collins stared at the dying campfire, the sky above him a showplace for brilliant stars. But he barely noticed them.

Once again, in spite of himself, he was

worried about Courtney. Had she really called her father? Or had she instead talked to one of the friends her father so disapproved of? Maybe she'd even called Nolan Ruggers. If that was so, she'd probably also engineered the plan to stay behind at the campsite so she could make her call.

Roger Collins's head spun from trying to figure Courtney out. And his headaches over Barry Cooper didn't help his state of mind, either. Barry was trying, and that counted for a lot as far as Mr. Collins was concerned, but things didn't seem to be getting any easier for the awkward, heavy-set boy. If anything, Bruce Patman's quips were getting harder and harder for him to take. And Bruce's comments had spawned an unofficial competition among some of the others to match his caustic wit. Barry was so slow on his bicycle that it was a wonder he made any progress at all, so clumsy that if someone heard something drop and break, he or she didn't even have to turn around to know that Barry was standing red-faced, sputtering half-intelligible apologies and excuses. And the pressure of knowing the others were watching him only aggravated Barry's ineptitude.

But he was by no means unintelligent, and no doubt he was aware of the laughter at his expense. More than once, Mr. Collins had caught him looking as if he was going to burst into tears any moment.

And as if there wasn't trouble enough, Bruce was still giving his cousin Roger a hard time, and Elizabeth—sweet, good-natured, one of Mr. Collins's favorite students—seemed awfully blue, though she was making an obvious effort to show a happy face. Mr. Collins couldn't help noticing that Todd was paying quite a bit of attention to Courtney lately.

Roger Collins was trying to handle the problem situations with the fairness and delicacy they required. He watched Courtney carefully, asking himself questions but trying not to jump to conclusions, and he soothed Barry's frazzled nerves with words of encouragement. He'd had a brief, yet firm, chat with Bruce about Barry and Roger, and he'd made sure Elizabeth knew she could come to him and talk if she needed to. But his heart wasn't where it used to be. It hadn't been since the day Nora Dalton had gone back to dating George Fowler.

That was an even bigger mystery than Courtney Thomas's sudden turnaround. Since that day, Mr. Collins couldn't figure out exactly how he felt about the petite French teacher. Fury, sorrow, affection, confusion—and every other feeling he had ever known—seemed to alternately ebb and flow inside him, creating clashing tides of emotion.

But one thing was clear. Nora Dalton was on Roger Collins's mind every minute of the day, every day of the week. And no matter what dark twists and turns his feelings about her took, just her voice or her face, or even the thought of her, was enough to turn the calm, rational Mr. Collins into a man who acted before he thought.

The sleeping bag incident was a perfect example. He'd told the kids that he wasn't going to nose about to find out who the culprit was, yet five minutes later he'd let his anger get the better of him, and he'd stormily confronted Lila Fowler. Perhaps she had been one of the responsible parties. Still, there would have been better, more gentle ways to deal with the whole thing. It was so unlike him to fly off the handle. But when Nora Dalton was involved, his reason seemed to melt like ice under a tropical sun.

Of course he'd apologized to Lila, but he was furious at himself for losing his cool with her in the first place. As a teacher and a trip leader, it was his responsibility to set an example, to be sympathetic, to be beyond reproach.

As the last embers of the camp fire faded to black, Roger Collins resolved to get Nora Dalton out of his system once and for all and to devote one-hundred percent of his energies to the kids on the trip. Because if his bleak premonition about the troubles ahead came true, some of the kids were going to need all the help he could give them to weather the storm.

Elizabeth pulled through the water with

smooth, graceful strokes, the water's warmth surrounding her like a velvet blanket. As she approached the shallow edge of the lake, she did a little dolphin dive and resurfaced a few yards away near the grassy shore.

Todd glided up alongside her. "Last one out's a rotten egg," he challenged.

They both sprinted out of the warm lake water into the pungent, cool night air, reaching their towels at the same instant.

Elizabeth dried off hurriedly, shivering a little as she wriggled into a warm, soft pair of blue sweat pants and pulled a matching sweat shirt over her damp bathing suit. "Mmm. That felt great. A perfect end to a perfect night."

Todd came up to her and slipped his powerful arms around her waist. "It was terrific, wasn't it?" He lowered his lips onto hers for a light kiss. "Well, except for Courtney, of course. It's really too bad she missed out on all the fun."

Just hearing her name roll off Todd's lips was enough to break the spell. Why did he insist on bringing her up right in the middle of their own private moment? Couldn't he stop thinking about her even for one evening? Suddenly the stars didn't seem as bright, nor the night so totally perfect. "Yeah, too bad, I guess." Elizabeth's voice was low.

Todd unwrapped his arms from around her. "Liz, why do I get the feeling you don't really mean that?'' His words were shaded with puzzlement.

"Do you?'' Elizabeth challenged, tension creeping into her body as once again the conversation focused on Courtney Thomas.

"Yes, I do,'' Todd said softly. "And I wish you would tell me why. It's so unlike you to hold a grudge against somebody for no reason at all. I just can't figure it out.''

"For no reason at all?'' Elizabeth echoed. In a flash the night seemed to have gone from crisply cool to ice cold. Her teeth chattered, and she hugged herself for warmth.

"For no reason I can see,'' Todd continued. "All I know is that my girlfriend, who's kind and helpful and loving, seems to have some weird grudge against a person she barely knows. What's the story, Liz? I wish you'd talk to me,'' he implored. "You know, Courtney needs some help from time to time, and I would have thought you'd be the first to volunteer it.''

Elizabeth felt the blood rush to her head. She had done everything in her power not to explode at Courtney when she draped herself all over Todd. But now that wasn't enough. Now Todd expected her to jump whenever Courtney said the word.

"Todd, she's getting enough help already!'' Elizabeth's words came out like a shot from a pistol. "From you. My boyfriend. Who spends all his time being loyal." She paused. "To another girl, that is!"

Todd sat down on the ground and sighed loudly. "Liz! This again? I thought we'd settled this the other night. I'm just trying to lend Courtney a hand. The way you help Barry. And you don't see me getting angry because you've stopped to help him adjust his brake cable or because you've offered to carry his share of the equipment when he was having trouble making it up some hill."

"That's different!" Frustration laced Elizabeth's protest. "That poor boy is trying so hard. And absolutely nobody's on his side. You know that's true. And, well, *someone* has to help him out." She lowered herself down onto the soft sand and faced Todd square on.

"Liz, don't you think Courtney needs a helping hand, too?" Todd countered. "Of all people, I wouldn't think you'd be the one to be fooled by her glittery image. Deep down, she's lived a sheltered life, always being taken care of by servants, shuttled to school and back in her father's limousine. In a way, this is her first time out in the real world. She's never done anything like this before."

"Do you really believe that?" Elizabeth's temper rose like a helium balloon. "How about that side of Courtney we saw those first two days? I'd hardly call that sheltered. I know she told us that her father hoped this trip would toughen

106

her up, but frankly, at that point she seemed tougher than everyone on this trip combined." Elizabeth inhaled deeply. "I think that if Courtney doesn't try to do things on her own, it's because she can get you to do them for her. It's a way of forging a cozy little bond between the two of you."

An uncomfortable silence filled the night. Finally Todd began speaking. "Liz, I really think you're judging Courtney unfairly. There are things about her you don't know—"

"Such as?" Elizabeth challenged.

"Such as the real reason why her father sent her on this trip. You're right in saying that it wasn't to toughen her up. That was just an excuse she invented to protect her father."

"Her father?" Elizabeth was confused.

"Yeah. She broke down and confessed it all to me the other night." Todd stretched out on his side, picking up handfuls of sand and sifting them through his fingers as he spoke. "Her father has a terrible drinking problem. I know it doesn't seem that way, but that's what makes it even worse. He drinks in secret. Alone. He has for years. So if Courtney's moods seem to switch kind of abruptly, you ought to be able to understand why. She's had a heck of a time growing up alone with an alcoholic father. Her mother died when she was just a kid.

"All Mr. Thomas's affection for Courtney," Todd continued. " 'Precious,' and 'dear,' and 'sweetheart'? It's just a show for guests. The real Steve Thomas has only two loves—his business and his booze. Courtney's had nobody to go to for attention or affection." Todd's voice was filled with sympathy. "Sometimes she feels so alone, so desperate, that she turns to people like Nolan Ruggers and his friends just for company."

Elizabeth listened in astonishment. Was it really possible? Outgoing, friendly, energetic Steve Thomas, who seemed to have everything in the world, was really a hopeless drunk? It was hard to swallow.

"It's true, Liz," Todd said. "The horror stories Courtney told me about when she was growing up—I wouldn't wish any of them on my worst enemy. And of course, Mr. Thomas doesn't really care if Courtney has fun on this trip. He just wants to get her out of his hair so he can hit the bottle whenever he feels like it."

Elizabeth tried to picture Mr. Thomas hiding inside his vast wood-and-glass palace, steadily emptying quart after quart of liquor. "Todd, I just don't see how a man in a position like his could keep such a big drinking problem secret. You saw for yourself what a busy schedule he has—always rushing off to meet some big star or other, the phone ringing constantly. And you mean to say that not one of the people he does business with is on to him? That his problem doesn't show in his work?"

"Liz, are you implying that Courtney is a liar?" Todd's words rushed out furiously. "Maybe she was right about you. She said she didn't think you liked her. But I told her, 'Just give Liz time. She's the friendliest, most sympathetic, big-hearted person, my Liz.' Yet all along . . . well, Courtney saw a side of you that I never realized was there."

Elizabeth felt the first tear trickle down her cheek. "I like to think I am sympathetic and bighearted," she said, sniffling. "But when someone's trying to take my boyfriend away from me—that's where I draw the line."

"Liz, why don't you believe me when I tell you that nobody's trying to take me away from you? The only thing that's going to get in the way of our relationship is if the sweet, wonderful girl I fell in love with has turned into someone who's uncompassionate and spiteful."

The dam burst, and hot, salty tears streamed down Elizabeth's face. "Do you really think that's what I've become?" she cried.

"I don't know." Todd's words were now a whisper of sorrow. "All I *do* know is that Courtney wants so much to be your friend."

Elizabeth waited for her tears to stop before replying. "Todd," she said tightly, "I really can't figure out what to make of this new story about Courtney's father. If it's true, then there are plenty of reasons to feel sorry for her. But if it's not, then she's even lower than I'd ever have guessed, spreading rumors about her own father for God knows what reason.''

Todd gave a loud, angry sigh at her last sentence, but Elizabeth continued to speak, her emotions simmering just under the surface of her words. ''But whatever the case, one thing's for sure. Courtney's more interested in making friends with you than with anyone else. Maybe she's been telling you that she'd like to get to know me, but I'll bet the truth is that she wouldn't mind in the least if I rode my bicycle off the edge of a cliff.''

Even as the words were leaving her mouth, they sounded hard and cold—as if they were coming from someone else. Elizabeth bit down hard on her lower lip. Jealousy and utter confusion over what was true and what was false about Courtney mingled with an icy, petrifying fear of losing the boy she loved. Her thoughts spun so wildly, she wasn't sure what she was feeling.

''So,'' Todd shot back, ''you've been taking behavior lessons from your sister.''

''And just what is that supposed to mean, Todd Wilkins?''

''It means that your mean, self-pitying comment sounds exactly like something Jessica would say.''

''Is that so?'' Rage shook Elizabeth's words. ''And just where do you get off attacking my sister like that? With the show Courtney put on back when we first met her, she makes Jessica look like the Good Samaritan!"

Todd's laughter coming through the dark was the last thing on earth that Elizabeth expected to hear. "I hadn't realized this argument was so amusing," she said angrily.

"Oh, Liz, I'm sorry," Todd sputtered, still laughing as he talked. "But I just had this image of Jessica stopping her bicycle in the middle of some out-of-the-way mountain road to help an old man across the street."

In spite of herself, Elizabeth smiled.

She began to giggle softly as she, too, pictured the scene in her mind's eye. "The noble Jessica, zooming along on her trusty bicycle, racing to the aid of people everywhere," she suggested.

"Faster than a speeding bullet," Todd recited, relaxing his shoulders, "more powerful than a locomotive . . ."

"It's Super-Jess!" they finished in unison.

"Sister of none other than Super-Liz," Todd added. "Super-Liz." His tone grew soft. "The girl I love. I really do." He put a tentative hand on her cheek.

Elizabeth tilted her face toward him. "And you don't think I'm—I'm uncompassionate and spiteful?" Just remembering Todd's angry exclamations hurt all over again.

"No, Liz. I apologize. I don't know how I could have said that about you. Look, I don't want to fight anymore, so let's just drop the sub-

111

ject of Courtney, OK? The last thing I want is for her to get between us—her or anyone else, for that matter." He gently drew Elizabeth toward him.

She accepted his kiss and put her arms around him. The air was warm and sweet again, and Elizabeth was sure the crickets on the banks of the lake were chirping their approval.

But as they headed back to the campsite, hoping nobody was worrying about what had happened to them, Elizabeth was left with a desperate feeling of unease. First, she didn't know what to believe about Courtney. Her confusion was worse than ever now, and it was impossible to gauge whether she should feel sorry for Courtney or keep an even sharper lookout for the girl's venomous intentions. And second, Elizabeth had a feeling that all was not said and done with Todd on the subject. His arm was draped lovingly around her now, but how many more times would either of them be content simply "to drop the subject"? It wasn't the first argument Elizabeth and Todd had had because of Courtney, and there was no reason to assume it would be the last.

Eight

Dear Cara,

Bionic Barry is even more of a loser than
that nerd, Theo. (Remember, in our math
class last year? The one with the plaid
polyester pants and the runny nose?) At
least Theo was a whiz with numbers. Barry
can't do anything right. Last night at dinner
he cut one of his fingers trying to crack open
a lobster claw! He must be the only person
in the history of the galaxy to get pinched by
a dead, cooked lobster!

Jessica snickered as she scribbled the opening
paragraph of her letter to Cara Walker. Her best
friend and fellow conspirator in countless
schemes, Cara, a junior counselor at a camp in
Oregon that summer, would certainly get a kick
out of the perils of Barry Cooper.

Anyway, just my luck, the big fat klutz decides to have a whopping crush on guess who? You got it. Nobody other than yours truly. Fortunately I can outride him, outrun him, outswim him, and do whatever else I have to to get a little peace.

Liz says he's probably fallen for me precisely because he knows it's an impossible fantasy. You know, like being in love with a movie star or something. Liz also says it's a harmless crush and that I ought to let the guy live, but yuck, Cara, just the thought of that ball of dough thinking he has the right to put me in his dreams at night makes me positively ill. I swear, Barry makes Winston look like some kind of Mr. Right.

Winston Egbert, the gangly clown of the Sweet Valley High junior class, had been head over heels in love with Jessica for just about forever. But Barry's obvious show of affection almost made Jessica long for Winston's antics.

The other real pain-in-the-neck of the group is Courtney Thomas, the daughter of Mr. Patman's friend who hosted us in L.A. Somehow Mr. Thomas got the bright idea of sending his precious darling along with us. Cara, you've got to see Courtney to believe her. And even then it's hard to know if the girl is for real. She started out as a real witch, too busy running around with her trashy boyfriend to even give us the time of day. Then somehow, very mysteriously, she transformed herself into a regular ray of sunshine. Just in time to enlist most of the kids on this trip to help her pitch her tent and repair her bicycle and just generally fawn all over her and make her feel like the star she seems to think she is.

What's absolutely incredible is that all she has to do is toss her mane of hair and smile, and everyone buys her act. Especially boys. And one in particular, even more than the rest. Guess who? None other than Liz's Mr. Wonderful—Todd Wilkins! Yup, you read it right, Cara. Hard to believe, but true. I honestly don't know what kind of spell she's got over that boy.

Liz is pretty miserable, even though she won't admit it. She keeps insisting that nothing's going on between those two, and she's even gone as far as defending Courtney. I keep telling her not to be so naive. She ought to just dump Todd. That's what he deserves. Liz is way too good for him. But she won't listen to me.

Jessica put her pen down for a moment and looked around for her twin. Elizabeth was sitting by her tent reading a book, while Todd was showing Courtney how to adjust the handlebars on her bicycle. Courtney was looking up at Todd, her eyes wide, as if he were explaining the most fascinating thing in the world.

"Somebody ought to give both Todd and Courtney a sound spanking!" Jessica wrote in bold letters.

But on to other topics! It looks like Charlie Markus and Annie Whitman are going to be a new couple, even though Bruce has made it clear that he disapproves. Bruce also still has it in for cousin Roger (surprise, surprise). Some things never change. But Olivia's helping Roger shoulder the hard feelings. They're the same disgustingly cozy couple they've always been.

And, speaking of romance, I saved the best news, the absolute best news, for last. His name is Robbie October. He's got curly, chestnut-brown hair, and the most incredible body. Cara, if you saw him, you'd be totally in love, too!

He and his brother are cycling along the coast, too, so we'll definitely be seeing a lot of each other. Maybe you'll even see him visiting me back in Sweet Valley after the summer!

Jessica didn't bother to tell Cara that she hadn't exactly met Robbie yet. Because it was really only a matter of time before she remedied that one little problem.

Well, that's all for now. I hope the boy counselors at your camp are as cute as Robbie. (I'll send you a picture of him as soon as I can.)

Love,
Jess

P.S. We have a mail stop coming up in another week, so WRITE!

Jessica folded the letter without rereading it and stuffed it into an envelope, which she tucked away in the side pocket of one of her saddlebags, until she would have a chance to get to a mailbox. As she grabbed her towel and headed down a narrow dirt path to the lake, Cara was quickly forgotten.

But not Robbie October. He was never far from Jessica's thoughts. Not when she was swimming, or lying in the sun, or during the group's afternoon visit to the local wharf, or their final cookout at the campground.

It wasn't that Jessica wasn't enjoying herself. On the contrary, the three-day stay in Santa Barbara had been terrific. But Jessica knew beyond a shadow of a doubt that as soon as Robbie turned up again things were going to get better still!

*   *   *

"Jess, hey, Jess, I've got to talk to you for a minute!" Lila burst into the kitchen of the hostel they had arrived at earlier in the afternoon.

"What?" Jessica yelled, swaying to the music on her Walkman while she mixed batter for chocolate-chip cookies.

"Jessica, there's something I have to tell you. It's important."

Jessica kept moving to a song that she alone could hear. "What's up?" Her voice echoed loudly in the quiet room.

Bruce Patman, chopping onions at Jessica's right, put his knife down just long enough to lift the earphones off Jessica's head. "Are you trying to make sure they hear you all the way back in Sweet Valley?" he asked sarcastically.

Jessica flashed him a venomous look. "Of all the people to get stuck on dinner duty with." Then she turned to Lila and smiled sweetly. "Now what was it you were going to tell me?"

"In private, Jess."

"Right now? I'm in the middle of something." Jessica measured out a cup of chopped walnuts and added them to her mix.

"It's about the plan," Lila hissed.

"Plan?" Jessica sounded slightly annoyed as she gave the batter a final stir.

Lila covered the side of her face with her hand

118

so that Bruce couldn't see her lips as she mouthed Courtney's name.

"Oh, *that* plan." Jessica pressed the off button on her Walkman and tossed aside the wooden spoon she'd been using. "Bruce, I'll be back in a minute. Just keep chopping. You can manage that, can't you?"

Bruce scowled as Jessica followed Lila out of the kitchen. "Next time I'm going to remember to bring my cook along when I go away," he mumbled.

Jessica sighed. "Honestly," she said when they were out of Bruce's earshot, "he's as bad in the kitchen as you are. What do you people do on the servants' night off, anyway?"

Lila looked Jessica straight in the eye. "Cold lobster and caviar," she said earnestly.

Jessica rolled her blue-green eyes. "I guess I had that coming to me. But, look, I can't leave Bruce alone in there too long, so what's happening?"

Now Lila looked down at her hands and fidgeted with the gold-and-ruby band around one of her fingers. "Jess, you know that scheme we came up with to make Courtney think this place is haunted?" Lila's voice was low.

"What about it? I already told Courtney that weird things have been happening here ever since a teenage girl vanished from this house without a trace a few years ago."

Lila sighed. "I was afraid of that."

119

"Afraid? What are you talking about?" Jessica said shrilly. "Courtney's the one who's supposed to be afraid, not you. I mean of course she pooh-poohed the whole thing, but when she feels something cold blowing across her face in the middle of the night and hears weird noises and scratching on the window near her bed, she's going to be singing another tune. Boy, is she going to look like a fool!"

Lila bit her lip. "What I meant, Jessica, is that I'm afraid I can't go through with it." Lila couldn't meet her friend's gaze.

"Lila, I thought we'd settled this already!"

"But I just heard something new about Courtney," Lila protested weakly. "And I changed my mind."

"You *can't* change your mind!" Jessica ordered. "I'm not going to be able to do all those spooky effects by myself. And now that I've started planting all those stories in Courtney's head, *I'll* look like a fool if we don't go through with the plan."

"Jessica, don't you even want to hear what made me change my mind?" Lila asked, starting to sound more sure of herself now.

"Lila, I've only got a minute," Jessica replied in exasperation, glancing back in the direction of the kitchen. "And I just want you to know that you're not going to get out of this so easily."

Lila grabbed her friend by the wrist. "Jessica,

120

hear me out," she insisted. "You might change your mind, too."

"I doubt it," Jessica answered, anger welling up inside her. She shook her arm free of Lila's grasp.

Lila inhaled sharply. "What would you say if you found out that there's a good reason why Courtney needs so much attention and help?"

"Of course there is," Jessica snapped. "The reason is that, number one, she's never had to do anything for herself before, and number two, she always has to be the center of attention."

"Jessica, it goes much deeper than that." Lila tossed her light-brown hair. "Courtney's had the kind of awful life you usually only read about in the newspapers."

"With all her money? I don't believe it for a second. Who's responsible for this story?"

"How about your own twin sister!"

Jessica was stunned. "Liz?"

"No, your other twin," Lila said sarcastically. "I overheard her telling Olivia . . ."

Jessica listened in astonishment as Lila recounted Courtney's life saga—Mr. Thomas's drinking problems, his daughter's unhappy childhood, the works. "Lila, how did Liz find all this out?" she asked finally, her words still edged with disbelief.

"She told Olivia that Courtney had confided in Todd," Lila answered.

"Ah-hah!" Jessica crowed triumphantly. "So

this all came down from the poor, pitiable Ms. Thomas herself. And you actually believe her?"

Lila's brow was furrowed. "As a matter of fact, Jess—"

"Later, Lila," Jessica broke in abruptly. Suddenly she was staring straight ahead as if in a trance. There in the hallway was Robbie October, looking even more handsome than he had the last time, in a forest green T-shirt and a pair of khaki pants. For a split second, Jessica was mesmerized. But she quickly snapped into action as she saw Robbie heading for the side door. Again. There was no way she could let him walk right out of her life a second time without even the vaguest idea that she was alive.

She began walking toward him.

Lila watched her friend close in on her target. "Hey, Jess, I thought you only had a minute!"

Jessica ignored her.

"What about Bruce?"

Jessica didn't bother to answer. Suddenly she let out an exclamation of delight. "Bart! Bart Templeton! Wow, you're the last person in the world I expected to see here." She ran up to Robbie and threw her arms around his neck.

"Um, excuse me," Robbie said. "I think you've got the wrong guy." His voice was deep and mellow.

Jessica pulled back, but not before she'd given him a long, hard hug, allowing herself to feel his muscles rippling beneath his shirt. Now she

122

looked into his eyes—green, rimmed with black. "Omigod! You're *not* Bart. I'm *so* sorry. Oh, how embarrassing!"

Robbie shrugged. "Don't worry about it," he told Jessica, moving past her toward the door.

Jessica hastily narrowed the gap between them again. "You don't know a guy named Bart who looks sort of like you?"

"What did you say his last name was?" Robbie stopped and regarded her.

"Templeman—I mean Templeton," Jessica said, correcting herself.

"Nope. My name's Robbie. Robbie October."

"Jessica Wakefield." She put on her best sultry smile and gazed into his eyes.

"Oh. Nice to know you, Jessica," Robbie replied perfunctorily as he turned toward the door once more.

"Um—uh—where are you going?" Jessica blurted out, desperate not to see Robbie disappear again.

Robbie gave Jessica a quizzical look. "I heard there was a good bar in the next town over. My brother's waiting for me outside. We thought we'd check it out. Do you know anything about it?"

"Well, no," Jessica admitted. "We—um—we just got here. Me and my group, that is. We haven't had a chance to find out much about what's around."

"Oh, you're with a group?" Robbie's lip

turned up in disdain. "I did a trip like that once. Never again. Too many rules and chores and people looking over your shoulder all the time."

"I know exactly what you mean." Jessica was eager to let Robbie know that playing by the rules wasn't her style either. "It's a real drag, isn't it?"

Robbie took a closer look at Jessica, his eyes traveling from her head right down to the tips of her sneakers. "If you let them push you around, it is."

"Well, of course I don't," Jessica was quick to insist. "I mean, if I wanted to go to that bar right now, I would."

Robbie looked amused. "Right now? With a total stranger?"

Jessica took a step nearer to Robbie. Her lips were only inches from his. "Is that an invitation?"

"That's what you wanted, wasn't it?" Robbie asked, arching an eyebrow. He was so near that Jessica could feel his breath on her face. Her heart beat crazily.

But her moment of blissful delirium was cut short by Bruce Patman's voice. "Jessica, can't you save your enchantress act until after dinner? The hamburgers are burning, and the cookie batter's not finished yet."

Jessica whipped around to face Bruce. Only Robbie's continued presence by her side kept her from exploding altogether. "Can't you see I'm busy? Look, Bruce, all you have to do is put a slice of cheese on each of the burgers and broil them for a few more minutes until it melts. The cookie batter just needs to be stirred up. Then you've got to drop it by teaspoons onto that baking sheet I got out."

"What about the onions? And the hamburger rolls, too. You know, I'm not supposed to be doing this all by myself while you practice your femme fatale act."

Jessica gritted her teeth. Next to her, Robbie tapped his foot impatiently. She looked up at his handsome face, then over at Bruce, whose arms were folded across his chest. From the kitchen came the smell of cooking hamburgers.

She tried to calculate her options. She could follow Bruce into the kitchen like a meek, obedient puppet, fulfilling her duties to her group. What would Robbie think of her then? Or she could go right out the door and leave Bruce staring after her. But then she'd have to contend with Mr. Collins and Ms. Dalton and the rest of them. That wouldn't be any picnic, either. In fact, they might even send her home. Back to Sweet Valley. And then she'd never see Robbie again.

She knew it was her own fault. She never should have boasted to Robbie about being able to walk out of the hostel any time she wanted to.

But while she berated herself, Robbie was going for the door for the third and final time.

"Jessica, maybe I'll catch you when the cooking lesson is over."

"Wait! Robbie, you don't understand . . ." Jessica threw her hands up in the air.

"Sure I do." Robbie pushed open the door. "The rules say you have to make dinner tonight, and there's nothing you can do about it. I know the whole story."

"Listen, if you just wait a few minutes, I can finish up quickly." Jessica's words were tinged with urgency. "I don't have to eat with the group, or anything. I just have to finish fixing the meal."

But Robbie was striding toward his brother, who was outside. "Jessica, it could've been fun," he called to her. "If you didn't have to deal with that whole group scene."

Jessica stood rooted in utter frustration as Robbie left, his brother with him. He didn't look back.

"Quite a performance," Lila offered. She was still standing exactly where Jessica had left her, a few feet away from the kitchen door.

"Oh, yeah. I forgot about you. The traitor," Jessica said darkly. Her face was a picture of distress and fury. It was all too much. First Lila giving up on their plan, then Robbie walking away from her a second time.

"I've been here for the whole show," Lila informed her sweetly. "In fact, I wouldn't have

126

missed it for anything. Bart Templeton, huh? That was a first-class piece of acting, Jess."

"For all the good it did me." Jessica's hands were clenched at her side.

Hey, don't be so hard on yourself," Lila said. "At least you get an A for effort."

"But you're going to get an F for dinner," put in Bruce, "if you don't do something about those burgers right now."

"Oh my gosh—the hamburgers." Jessica raced into the kitchen, Bruce and Lila trailing behind her. She pulled open the oven broiler to find a half-dozen blackened patties.

"Damn!" exclaimed Bruce. "Just because you had to go running after Mr. Muscles, Jessica."

Jessica spun around to face Bruce. "Just because *you* can't even boil water! Robbie's absolutely right about group trips. There's nothing fun about having to share your vacation with a bunch of incompetent idiots!"

"Oh, so now I'm an idiot?" Bruce gave Jessica a well-practiced sneer. "*You're* the jerk who went and threw herself all over some guy who obviously couldn't care less about her."

Jessica sank down into one of the kitchen chairs. "It's true, isn't it?" Suddenly Jessica felt the anger drain out of her, until all that was left was a horrible, dull ache in the pit of her stomach. As painful as it was to admit it, Bruce's words rang true.

Bruce stared at Jessica as if she had just grown

a second head. "Why bother?" Jessica continued. "It's not going to win me any points with Robbie. I blew it with him. I made a total fool out of myself, didn't I?"

Bruce and Lila exchanged incredulous glances. It was rare to see Jessica so defeated. "Hey," Bruce said softly, "I didn't think you were going to take it to heart like that. Come on. Where's the Jessica Wakefield fighting spirit we all love to hate?"

Jessica looked up at Bruce moist-eyed. "I know you're trying to make me laugh, Bruce. And I appreciate it. But my spirit just went out that door." She made a vague motion toward the side door of the hostel.

Lila bent down and put a hand on her friend's knee. "Don't give up, Jessica."

Jessica scowled as she pushed Lila's hand away. "You! You're just trying to be nice to me so I won't be mad about how you backed out of our plan. I'll bet you couldn't care less about Robbie and me."

"Oh, come on, Jess. One thing has nothing to do with the other. I really think you shouldn't get so down on yourself. Everyone's allowed to strike out once in a while. Even you. There are plenty of other boys. Maybe next time you'll hit a home run!"

But Jessica remained despondent. As she'd told Lila before, she didn't want any other boys. She wanted Robbie; her heart was set on it. It was as simple as that. She moved listlessly around the kitchen, scraping the tops of the charred burgers, doctoring them with a topping of onions and cheese, and making fresh patties out of the remaining ground meat.

Bruce was as sweet as pecan pie for the next half hour, doing everything Jessica asked him to, without a single snide word or complaint. Lila even offered to help with the salad.

In the end, the meal was a big success. But Jessica remained shadowed in a cloud of angry despair. Having Lila go over to Courtney's camp was bad enough. But the scene with Robbie had been the clincher. She'd approached Robbie with her arms wide open, and for one jubilant moment, it had seemed that he was hers. But in the blink of an eye, her hopes had been dashed. Over and over, Jessica recalled Robbie walking away, without so much as a backward glance.

Nine

Lila sat on the couch in the common room of the hostel, a pad of notepaper in her lap, her pen uncapped and poised in the air. But she wasn't writing anything. She was listening to the two boys on her left, huddled over the latest issue of *Sports Illustrated*.

She sneaked a peek at them, especially at the lanky blond, as she tried to figure out a good opening line to use. It was too bad Jessica wasn't around to help her out. Jessica was the unequivocal master of opening lines. But she had gone to bed early with an advanced case of the grouchies, too angry at Lila to say a proper goodnight and too heartbroken over Robbie to bother saying an improper one.

So Lila was on her own. She inched closer to the boys, listening to their conversation.

"Don, check out his article on racing bikes,"

the blond boy said. "Boy, would I like to have one of these babies."

"Wouldn't do you much good on a trip like this," the other boy replied. "No rear rack for your bags, tires that couldn't stand up to the roads we've been riding on, not even any brakes!"

"No brakes?" The words were out of Lila's mouth before she realized it.

The two boys turned toward Lila as she clapped a hand over her mouth, her face turning a deep shade of red. "I'm really sorry," she finally managed. "But I just couldn't help over-hearing your discussion."

The blond boy laughed and gave a little wave of his hand. "Hey, don't worry about it. I'm with you. The idea of a bicycle without brakes *is* pretty weird."

Lila let out a tiny sigh of relief. For a minute there, she thought she'd blown her chances with them by such obvious eavesdropping.

"You have to understand that it's to make the bikes as light as possible," Don explained. "These might not be ideal for touring," he con-tinued, gesturing at the pictures in *Sports Illustrated*, "but for racing, they can't be beat." He passed the magazine over to Lila so she could examine the color illustrations.

Lila took the opportunity to edge nearer to her two new friends, feigning great interest in the racing bicycles. Maybe her slip hadn't been such a big mistake after all. "Pretty sleek machines," she commented, eyeing the blond boy, with his chocolate-brown eyes and warm smile.

He grinned at her, a dimple in his left cheek. "By the way," he said, "I'm Pat, and this is my friend Don. Our group is headed up to the Sierras. We're doing a combined biking-hiking trip."

"Sounds great," Lila said enthusiastically, returning Pat's grin with her own best smile. "My name's Lila. I'm with the Sweet Valley group, cycling up the coast."

"Oh, yeah. I saw you people come in earlier," said Don. "Say, isn't your leader that pretty black-haired woman?"

Lila cringed. Why did that woman haunt her everyplace she went? "We have two leaders," Lila replied guardedly. "And, yes, Nora Dalton is one of them." She spoke the French teacher's name through clenched teeth.

Pat and Don exchanged curious glances. "Nora Dalton?" Pat echoed, puzzlement tinting his words. "Strange. She looks exactly like Beth Curtis, this woman who used to teach at the high school we go to, in Arizona. She disappeared about a year and a half ago."

Lila felt every muscle in her body tense up. Nora Dalton had arrived in Sweet Valley at just about that time. And she had revealed little about herself and even less about where she had come from. Was it possible that this chance meeting was the key to Ms. Dalton's mysterious past? Lila gripped the arm of the couch. "What did Beth Curtis teach?" she asked, feeling a sharp tingle of nervous anticipation as she formed the question.

"French."

Lila gasped. The single syllable Pat had uttered was like a gold mine to her. Suddenly there was more at stake than just a boy with a cute face and his friend. There would be plenty of good-looking guys to get to know as the group made their way north toward San Francisco, but the opportunity to unravel Ms. Dalton's well-guarded secrets was the chance of a lifetime.

"Tell me, Pat," she said, "what else do you know about Beth Curtis?"

" 'Off the coast highway, nestled in the valley of the Santa Ynoz River,' " Elizabeth read out loud, " 'lies the town of Lompoc, whose miles upon miles of flower beds produce half of the grown flower seeds in the world.' " She shut the guidebook. "Sounds absolutely beautiful," she said. "That's my vote for tonight's stop."

Mr. Collins studied the map he'd laid out on one of the tables of the hostel's large dining room. He traced roads with the index finger of his right hand, pausing to lift his coffee cup to his lips with his free hand. "Hmm, here we are. Lompoc. Yup. Right here." He jabbed at a spot on the map for emphasis. "Right smack between here and Pismo."

"Halfway to our next scheduled stop, and pretty, too, huh? Sounds good to me," put in Roger Patman. "I cast my vote with Liz."

"Me, too," added Todd. "Because we all know what good taste Liz has." He flashed a put-on toothy grin, as several of the kids giggled at his joke.

"What do you say, gang?" asked Mr. Collins. "Should we make today's phantom stopover in Lompoc?"

A chorus of approval answered his question.

No one was disappointed later that afternoon when they approached the vast, brilliantly colored fields of flowers outside the town. Pink, purple, and red, each field seemed brighter and more awesome than the one before it. Stopping to rest by a plot of dazzling gold and orange calendulas, Elizabeth inhaled deeply, until she felt as if her lungs might burst from the sweet, perfumed air that filled them.

"Mmm! What do you say we pitch our tents right here," she suggested to Mr. Collins, who had pulled up next to her. "Can you imagine waking up to this in the morning?" But then she shook her head and laughed. "Though I guess there must be all kinds of rules about sleeping on the side of the road."

"I'm afraid so," the handsome trip leader confirmed. "But maybe waking up next to a flower field isn't as impossible as it sounds. I remember when I was in college, I made a trip cross-country with a couple of my buddies . . ."

Elizabeth grinned as she leaned against her sleek blue bicycle. She loved hearing about Mr. Collins's years at New York City's Columbia University. Sometimes, back at school, as the staff of *The Oracle* was putting together the latest issue of the Sweet Valley High newspaper, Mr. Collins, the paper's adviser, would entertain them with stories about wild fraternity parties, campus demonstrations, or nights out in the big city. His boyish enthusiasm as he told his tales made it easy to picture him as an adventurous man-about-campus.

Now his face lit up as he reminisced about his coast-to-coast trip. "It was the first time I saw the Pacific Ocean. I knew then that one day I wanted to settle down in California for good." He paused. "Anyway, we had an old beat-up Rambler. The White Stallion, we called it. Always breaking down, getting flat ties, you name it. So one day it conked out on us in the middle of Iowa, on a tiny back road. There was nothing around for miles but grass and cornfields. And it was getting late." Mr. Collins lowered his voice in a dramatic embellishment to his story. Elizabeth giggled along with some of the other kids who had gathered to hear what Mr. Collins was saying.

"Well my roommate, Tim—he's a big-shot television executive now—hitched a ride to the nearest gas station. Closed until the next morning. Of course there wasn't a chance of finding a motel in the area. Besides, we had the dead White Stallion on our hands, and it wasn't going to budge an inch until that garage opened again and sent out a tow truck." Mr. Collins wrinkled his forehead as if he were worrying that very moment about where he and his friends were going to spend the night.

"Hey, Mr. Collins," said Charlie, his arm solidly around Annie Whitman's slender waist. "You tell a good story, but what does this have to do with us finding a place to sleep tonight?"

"Markus, let the guy finish, will you?" Todd chided good-naturedly. "I'll bet you're the kind of kid who peeks at the last page of your book before you're finished, too."

Charlie hung his head in mock humiliation. "Guilty as charged," he said. "Sorry, Mr. Collins. Go ahead."

"Thank you, Charlie. As I was saying, it looked as if we were going to have to steel ourselves for a long night trying to catch some sleep in the White Stallion. But just as the sun was starting to disappear, an old man drove by us in a pickup truck and stopped to see if we were OK.

"Well, to make a long story short just for our friend Charlie here,"—Mr. Collins winked in Charlie's direction—"the guy owned a farm just up the road from where we'd broken down. We ended up sleeping in his barn for several days while repairs were being made on the car, and we baled hay for him a few mornings in return."

"So do you mean you think *we* can find a barn to stay in?" asked Elizabeth. "Where we can wake up to—this?" she gestured to the flowers around her.

"We can certainly try," answered Mr. Collins. "I saw a few back there,"—he pointed—"by some of those first fields. Besides, we ought to round up the rest of the gang and figure out where we're going to sleep while there's still plenty of daylight left."

A few hours later, the group was comfortably settled in.

"Not exactly the old wooden barn we expected, is it?" said Todd.

"Something even better," Elizabeth replied, leaning on his shoulder and feeling the thick wool of his sweater against her cheek. Through the glass panes of the one-time greenhouse, she watched the last streaks of flaming color in the sky as they faded into the deep blue, star-filled night.

"Three cheers for Mrs. Ames and her greenhouse," Todd whispered in Elizabeth's ear. Snuggling even closer to her, he planted a row of soft kisses across her cheek toward her mouth.

As their lips parted, Elizabeth sighed contentedly. When they broke away, Todd held Elizabeth close as he hummed along with the guitar Olivia had brought with her. On the other side of the old greenhouse, several of the kids sat around Olivia in a circle, singing as she strummed. Elizabeth felt cozy and warm. Even Mr. Collins couldn't have predicted just how well his plan of knocking on local doors was going to turn out.

Elizabeth and Annie had volunteered to knock on the first door, at a white, shuttered house. It was opened by a tiny, round-faced old woman who introduced herself as Nettie Ames. The laugh lines around her mouth deepened, and she giggled like a schoolgirl when Annie mentioned baling hay and sleeping in barns.

"My dear," Mrs. Ames had said, chuckling, "I'm afraid you're going to have to look awfully hard to find hay for baling or cows for milking. True, this is farm country, but we feed our flowers with pure California sunshine."

Annie's expression had instantly turned glum, and Elizabeth felt a bit depressed, too.

"Oh, but dear girls, don't look so blue," Mrs. Ames added quickly. "I do have one or two chores I need done around the little flower shop I run. And you and your friends might be very comfortable staying over in the old greenhouse near my ageratum field."

Elizabeth's brow furrowed.

"Ageratums. Those blue flowers," the old

woman explained, pointing toward the neatly planted rows that stretched out to one side of her house.

Elizabeth followed the direction of Mrs. Ames's finger until she spotted a rectangular palace of glass.

Now, nestled in Todd's arms, she looked from the inside out. The Big Dipper seemed to be pouring its nighttime magic right onto her. It had to be a good sign. Elizabeth crossed her fingers and wished with all her might that the good feeling would last.

"Lila, what do you want to talk to me about?" Nora Dalton's voice floated through the sweet-smelling night air. From inside the greenhouse came the faint strains of "Blowin' in the Wind."

"Doesn't that girl know anything but folk songs?" Lila asked, not bothering to respond to Ms. Dalton's question. She would drop her bombshell when she was good and ready. No sooner. The French teacher was going to have to learn who was in control now.

"Don't you enjoy Olivia's singing?" Ms. Dalton said guardedly.

She's nervous, thought Lila. *Wonderful. Just as it should be.* "No, I like new music. I can't be bothered with anything that's more than—oh, say a year and a half old," she said with studied casualness. A year and a half ago was when Ms. Dalton had come to Sweet Valley.

An expression of fear flitted across Nora Dalton's small, even features. "New music is great," she responded, making an obvious effort to keep her voice level, "but there's something to be said for oldies but goodies, too, wouldn't you say?"

"I'd say," began Lila, "that I really expected you, of all people, to be awfully keen on burying the past."

From a nearby hedge came the rustling sound of a bird or small animal. But Nora Dalton didn't look over to see what it was. In fact, she didn't move a muscle. Neither did Lila. They held each other's gaze in confrontation. The corners of Ms. Dalton's mouth turned down.

"So which is it?" Lila hammered away, never taking her eyes off the young French teacher. "Do you long for the past, or do you want to forget all about it?"

Nora Dalton's bottom lip began to tremble, and she wrapped her arms around herself, even though the night air was warm. "What are you trying to say?" Her voice was barely more than a whisper now.

"I'm trying to say that you meet all kinds of interesting people on these trips," Lila answered. By the ominous note in her voice, she let it be known that she wasn't simply making conversation. Ms. Dalton was silent. "In fact,"

Lila continued, "I met someone who knows you. But, funny, he seemed to think your name was"—she paused for effect—"Beth Curtis!"

Nora Dalton's strangled gasp was all the proof Lila needed. A slow, sly smile spread across her face. She had Ms. Dalton, or rather, Ms. Curtis, right where she wanted her.

Ten

Elizabeth awoke to the sound of someone crying. Her sleeping bag rustled faintly as she rolled over onto her stomach and lifted her head. She blinked hard, trying to focus her gaze in the waning moonlight that trickled into the greenhouse. The sobbing continued. It was a girl—Elizabeth could tell that much—and someone who lay not too far away, on the other side of where Todd was sleeping. Courtney. Courtney had rolled out of her sleeping bag right next to him, as close as she could.

The sobs were punctuated by sniffles. In a flash everything Todd had recounted about Courtney's problems came rushing into Elizabeth's head. What if it was all true? Suppose Courtney really did have every reason to cry in the middle of the night?

Elizabeth felt a sharp stab of guilt. Here she had been wishing that Courtney would just shrivel up and disappear, when all along the girl had truly needed all the support and friendship she could get. Elizabeth began to crawl out of her sleeping bag, taking care to be as quiet as possible. She didn't want to wake anyone else up. But as she extended her arms out of the bag, she was stopped by a voice. Todd's voice.

"Courtney?" he asked softly. Elizabeth froze. "Courtney, are you OK?"

The crying let up. "Todd? Is that you?" Courtney whispered, her voice still shaky. "Oh, Todd, I'm so worried about Daddy. I had the most awful dream."

Quick as a rocket, Todd was sitting up. Out of the corner of her eye, Elizabeth could see him stroking her hair. "Shh, Courtney. It's OK. It's going to be all right," he consoled her.

Elizabeth slid back down into her sleeping bag—stealthily, silently, so as not to attract their attention. Courtney didn't need her help. It was just as she'd told Todd the other evening, down at the campground lake. Courtney wanted Todd, and Todd alone.

Elizabeth buried herself deeper in the folds of her bag until Todd and Courtney's voices were nothing more than low murmurs. She felt as if her emotions were having a full-scale tug-of-war. One side of her felt sorry for Courtney, sorry for anyone who woke up sobbing her heart out. That side of Elizabeth wanted to reach out, to say to Courtney, "I'm here if you need me."

But that side was continuously being squelched by the other side, the side that was convinced that there was no alcoholic father in Courtney's life, that there were no problems at home—nothing but a very clever plan to turn Todd into her one-man fan club. Coaxed by the infamous green-eyed monster, jealousy, this side seemed to be winning out.

That only made Elizabeth feel worse. A tear slid down the side of her cheek. Was she really becoming the callous, insensitive person Todd had talked about down by the lake?

She peeped out from under her covers. Courtney and Todd were still now, and the only sound came from the chirping crickets outside the greenhouse. How was Elizabeth supposed to know which side of herself to listen to? If she didn't make the right decision, she risked losing the boy she loved.

She ached all over as she studied her boyfriend, his chest rising and falling rhythmically as he slept again. He looked so peaceful. She watched the way the moonlight played across his locks of wavy, dark hair. She couldn't lose him! She mustn't!

She inched closer to him. She needed to feel his steady, even breathing on her face. And then she noticed something that made her blood run cold. One of Todd's arms was stretched outside his sleeping bag, his fingers intertwined with Courtney's.

Elizabeth swallowed hard against the lump in her throat. At that moment the side of her that felt sorry for Courtney had all but vanished. At that moment she knew that Jessica had been right. She *was* too forgiving, too *naive*.

What kind of two-timing game was Todd playing? Elizabeth wondered in dread. Were all his kisses earlier that evening nothing but a big hoax? She clenched her teeth to hold back the threatening hurricane of tears. But it was no use.

Courtney's cries had been soothed away by Todd, but nobody heard Elizabeth. Her face was smothered against the sweat shirt she was using for a pillow. She finally surrendered to a fitful sleep, images of interlaced fingers piercing her dreams, her drenched sweat shirt pressed against her cheek.

"Boy, wasn't it swell of Mrs. Ames to cook waffles for the whole bunch of us?" Barry Cooper asked enthusiastically, his eyes never leaving Jessica's face as he dried a large frying pan.

"Barry, no one says 'swell' anymore," Jessica responded grumpily, swirling a pot around in the icy cold water of the stream behind Mrs. Ames's flower fields. "Where'd you pick that expression up anyway? Watching reruns of 'The Brady Bunch'?"

Barry turned as red as the bandanna he was

using as a dish towel. "Well—um—it was—uh—nice of her anyway," he mumbled meekly.

"And you can wipe that pathetic look off your face, too," Jessica added. "It won't do any good." She thrust the pot into Barry's hand. "I just don't feel like being sympathetic today. Get it?" Of all the mornings to get stuck doing dishes with Bionic Barry, Jessica thought, it would have to be when she felt about as low as a Munchkin in a submarine. On a day like that, the only smart thing to do was to crawl into bed and stay there. If she'd had a bed.

There was the entire problem. No bed, no place that was home for more than a night or two. Always a reason to get up, always someplace to go. And worst of all, always with the same lousy bunch of people. Like this jerk of all jerks, Barry. No matter how hard Jessica was on him, he never gave up. And Courtney. And that traitor, Lila. Especially Lila. Jessica had to admit it. She felt rotten.

"Jessica, what's wrong? Is there something I can do?" Barry asked.

Right! Jessica thought cynically. *There's really a lot you can do about the fact that my one friend on this trip has defected to the other side.* She pouted as she remembered how chummy Lila and Courtney had been the night before. "No, you wouldn't understand," she told Barry.

"Jessica, why won't you let me be your friend?" he asked sadly, his words barely audible. He nervously twisted his damp bandanna in his hands.

Jessica grimaced. "I know things are bad when you're the only friend I've got around here," she muttered under her breath.

"What, Jessica?" Barry asked.

"Oh, never mind," Jessica snapped. Why even waste her breath teasing a nerd like Barry? She finished cleaning the last pot and gave Barry a not-so-gentle nudge with it.

He reached out to take it, but Jessica released her grasp a second too soon. Barry's fingers slipped from the handle, and the pot fell into the stream with a loud splash.

"Oh, gosh, Jessica, I'm so sorry!" Barry immediately plunged his hand into the cold water and began groping about clumsily.

"Oh, I'll do it." Jessica's exasperation was obvious as she snatched the pot out of the stream. "Yuck, it's got mud all over it."

"Here, I'll wash it," Barry volunteered.

"Barry, the best kind of help from you is no help at all," Jessica informed him. "So why don't you just run along. I'll dry it, too."

"You don't have to, Jess, really. I don't mind at all. . . . I mean, I'd like to do you the favor—"

"Barry!" Jessica was almost yelling now. "You can do me the biggest favor of all by getting lost."

Barry's face wrinkled up as if he were on the verge of tears.

"Hey, look, don't take it so personally." Jessica softened her voice a little. The last thing she needed was to get stuck with a blubbering Barry on her hands. "I just need a few minutes alone, OK?"

Barry stared down at his hands, knotting and unknotting his bandanna. "OK," he said dejectedly. Jessica watched him waddle away.

She gave the pot a few careless wipes with her own bandanna, then put it on the ground next to her. Lying back on the grass, she sighed deeply. Above her, the sky was as blue as a robin's egg, and the sun shone brightly. The smell of fresh flowers and newly mown grass was like fine perfume. Yet everything felt wrong.

Jessica had to face the facts. Sure, she was upset about Lila. And it certainly wasn't any fun having Barry padding around after her everywhere she went, like a distorted shadow. But that wasn't the real problem. No, the real problem could be summed up in a six-letter word beginning with R, a word that conjured up images of broad shoulders, chestnut-colored curls, and the sound of a rich, sexy baritone with a hint of a West Coast twang.

Jessica pounded her fist against the dew-soaked earth. She'd blown it with Robbie again! Strike two! One more strike, and Jessica Wakefield would be O-U-T. If she even got another chance with him—and if she wasn't already out, as far as he was concerned. Why

148

hadn't she just gone with him the other night? What was a bunch of burned hamburgers compared with true love? What good was loyalty to her tripmates when the whole lot of them wasn't worth one Robbie?

She sat up and watched from a distance as the rest of the group hurried around, packing the backs of their bicycles and getting ready for the day's ride. Ugh. A day just like all the other days: pedaling, sweating, stopping for a quick break, and pedaling some more, struggling to get up all those hills and then coasting down the other side in no time flat. The easy parts were finished almost before they'd begun.

Sometimes Jessica wanted nothing more than to take her bicycle, throw it over the nearest cliff, and hop onto the first bus back to Sweet Valley—or to anywhere, for that matter. And for this she had given up the opportunity to spend an evening with the guy of her dreams?

"Jessica! Planet Earth to Jessica Wakefield!" Mr. Collins's voice cut into her thoughts. "Jess, I know it's lovely here, but I don't think you want to be left behind, do you?" he called.

"What do I care?" Jessica said sullenly to herself. But she stacked the pots, the pan, and the rest of the cooking utensils and slowly got up.

She found Lila strapping her sleeping bag onto her bicycle. "Hi, Jess!" Lila's greeting was so warm it seemed it had been years, and not mere minutes, since they'd last seen each other.

"You can forget the cherished-friend routine," Jessica said flatly. "It won't work."

"What on earth are you talking about?" Lila asked sweetly.

"You know very well, Ms. Lila Benedict Arnold Fowler. I saw you all buddy-buddy with Courtney last night."

"Oh, come on, Jess. Have a heart. Poor Courtney's had a terrible time of it."

"For starters, Lila, I wouldn't exactly call her poor. Did I forget to mention the last time we discussed her that her favorite gold ring is much more expensive looking than yours?"

"It won't work a second time, Jessica. I'm not competing against Courtney anymore." Lila was firm. "And if you'd just open up a little, you might even discover that she's not so bad. You know, the three of us could really be friends."

"Look, if you've fallen for her tricks, that's your problem," Jessica said coldly. "But don't drag me into it. I only came over here to give you the pots. It *is* your turn to take them, isn't it?" She took a certain amount of satisfaction in setting the pots down next to Lila's bicycle. Everyone agreed that carrying them was the worst of all possible chores, since they were so bulky and heavy.

"Gee, thanks for nothing," Lila replied sarcastically. She bent down to get the pots. But before her fingers reached them, she straightened back up, a funny gleam in her eye. "You know,

Jessica, on second thought, I don't think it *is* my turn."

"What are you talking about?" Jessica scowled.

"In fact, I'm quite sure it's Ms. Dalton's turn," Lila continued. "Isn't that right?" she said loudly as the tall, slender teacher walked by.

At the sound of Lila's voice, Ms. Dalton whipped around as if she'd been stung. "Excuse me, Lila? Did you say something to me?" Jessica couldn't miss her trip leader's timid manner.

"I was just telling Jessica that it's your day to carry the pots, *Ms. Dalton*." The way Lila spoke that name sent a little shiver of electricity up Jessica's spine, as if those two words were charged with some hidden meaning that only Lila and Ms. Dalton understood.

Jessica regarded the two of them quizzically. They were locked in a silent staring contest, aware, at that second, only of each other. Finally Ms. Dalton lowered her gaze to the ground and nodded slowly. "I guess you're right." Her voice was barely louder than a whisper.

"I knew you'd see it my way," Lila responded smugly, folding her arms across her chest.

Mystified, Jessica watched as Nora Dalton picked up the pots and loaded them onto her bicycle. There was no question in Jessica's mind that it was Lila's turn to carry the cookware. What was going on here?

Jessica wasn't the only one who was wondering. Roger Collins came over, a questioning look on his face. "Lila, that's your responsibility today," he announced.

"Mr. Collins, I think you're wrong," Lila replied in her sweetest voice. "Ms. Dalton here just agreed that it's her turn."

Nora Dalton nodded wearily, the color draining from her face. "She's right, Roger."

"But, Nora, you just carried them a few days ago." Mr. Collins looked from Ms. Dalton to Lila and then back again.

"Look, don't you think I know what I'm supposed to do?" Ms. Dalton snapped with uncharacteristic harshness. "Or do you think I need a leader, too?"

Mr. Collins reacted as if he'd been slapped in the face. Without a word, he turned and walked away.

Now Jessica was more curious than ever. What mysterious power did Lila have over Ms. Dalton? Jessica had an overwhelming urge to take Lila aside and get the whole story. Obviously *something* big was going on.

But at that moment Courtney emerged from the greenhouse, glanced over in Lila's direction, and waved. Lila gave an enthusiastic wave back.

Jessica's desire to have a chat with Lila deflated like a punctured balloon. Let Lila play her games with Courtney and Ms. Dalton and all the rest of them. What difference could it make to Jessica anyway?

The blue mood that had haunted her all morning increased. Jessica had no use for traitors like Lila or fakers like Courtney, not to mention misfits like Barry, or any of the other losers on this trip. She should have gone with Robbie when she'd had the chance. She kicked at a pebble as she made her way over to her bicycle. The rest of the vacation stretched out mercilessly before her—a long, dreary road with no end in sight.

"Liz, why won't you talk to me?"

Elizabeth was standing at a picnic table, concentrating on slicing tomatoes. She tried to block out Todd's familiar voice, but it was like trying to ignore the loud beating of her own heart.

"Liz, please," Todd implored again. He came up beside her and laid a hand on her shoulder.

His touch was like an electric shock. Elizabeth put the vegetable knife down on the table but didn't turn around. "Yes?" She couldn't see him, but she could feel his presence.

"Tell me what I did, Elizabeth. Liz." He reached out with his other hand and gently turned her around.

She looked up into his face—the face she'd loved for so long. Todd was her best friend, the boy who understood her almost as well as she understood herself. At least she'd thought he did. A tear glistened in the corner of her eye.

Todd reached up and wiped the tear away, his fingers brushing her cheek. "What is it?"

Elizabeth bristled and took a step backward. "You know." Her voice trembled.

"Liz, I don't."

Elizabeth shook her head, her anger mingled with despair. "Last night. Courtney." Her words sounded foreign to her ears, as if they belonged to someone else. "I—saw what happened."

Todd's expression of concern vanished. "Liz, I'm beginning to feel a little like a recording, saying the same thing over and over. Courtney's my friend. And she's going to stay my friend. If she needs my help, I'm going to be sure to give it to her."

"You've certainly made that plain enough," Elizabeth replied, clenching her fists to keep from unleashing a flood of tears.

Todd shook his head. "I just don't get it, Liz. You've never minded it before when I had friends who were girls. Just like I've never had problems with your male friends. No jealousy. I mean, why should there be? We've always known how special we were to each other." His voice softened. "Liz . . ." He stretched his hand toward her.

"No, Todd. We're not going to kiss and make up this time." Elizabeth sat down at the picnic table at the campsite they had reached that afternoon.

Todd sat down on the bench opposite her. "I don't see why it's any different than my being friends with Emily Mayer, for instance, or you're being friends with, say, Ken Matthews."

"Todd, can't you see I'm trying to make dinner?" Elizabeth broke several cloves off a bulb of garlic and started to peel them. "I told Annie I'd have all this stuff chopped by the time she came back from the supermarket." She set to work busily, never once looking up at Todd.

"Liz, since when is a lousy pot of spaghetti sauce more important than you and me? I mean, after all the time we've been together, I think I deserve some answers." Todd pounded his fist on the weatherbeaten wooden table. "So tell me. Why is Courtney any different from Emily or Ken? Why?"

"Because," Elizabeth finally exploded, all her fears, all her fury surfacing, "you've never woken up in the middle of the night to see me asleep next to Ken, my hand in his." Her voice rose as her words came out in a jumbled rush of anger.

Todd sighed angrily. "That's because you've never woken up to Ken crying like his heart might break. That's because Ken doesn't have a father he has to worry about every second of the day and night." Todd's tone matched Elizabeth's as he enumerated his reasons on his fingers. "And that's because Ken's got plenty of friends who won't let him down."

"Todd, maybe you think you've got all the answers, but as far as I'm concerned, there's a line between a friend and a girlfriend. And last night you stepped over that line."

"So you think I should have left Courtney to cry by herself. Is that it?" Todd bent down and picked a twig off the ground, then snapped it in two. "How about a little sensitivity? Or don't you know what that means anymore?"

Elizabeth took a deep breath and counted silently to ten. She had to be calm. Calm and rational. Otherwise, she might end up saying something she'd regret later. "Todd, I want you to try to imagine how you'd feel if you saw me sleeping hand in hand with another boy. Any boy other than you." Elizabeth couldn't even picture it herself. All through the past year at school it had been Todd and Elizabeth, Elizabeth and Todd. She couldn't imagine her name linked with anyone else's.

For a moment, it looked as if Todd was coming around. But Elizabeth's sigh of relief was premature. "Still, it wasn't any old person," Todd insisted. "It was somebody who really needed a comforting hand. Literally, I guess."

Elizabeth felt the heat rushing to her face again. "And where do I fit in? Am I just supposed to grin and bear it? I don't know what your definition of 'sensitivity' is, Todd Wilkins, but I could sure use a little of it now, too."

"Maybe you'd get some, Liz, if you'd give some."

Todd's words were an arrow shot straight at her heart. Elizabeth dropped her face into her hands, as if by blocking out the sight of the boy in front of her, she could block out his harsh, accusing words. She couldn't go on this way. No relationship at all would be better than the painful, twisted one she and Todd had been having ever since Courtney Thomas had come into their lives.

When she looked up again, her expression was set, her mouth a hard, tight line. "Todd, we can't seem to resolve anything. So maybe it's time to end things between us." Her voice was steady, toneless. Elizabeth knew that if she allowed herself even a split second of emotion, she would find herself drowning in a turbulent flood of hopelessness and misery.

"Is that what you want?" Todd's own words had a new hardness to them.

Elizabeth nodded. She couldn't trust herself to utter another sound.

Todd swallowed hard. "Then I won't argue with you about it." He turned on his heel and walked away.

Elizabeth's whole body shook, and the dam of emotion burst. Now the tears rushed out, a raging river that felt as if it would never stop.

Eleven

Elizabeth was just drying her tears when a moist-eyed Annie Whitman approached the picnic table, her arms laden with groceries. "Annie! What's the matter?" Elizabeth took the bags from her as Annie dropped down onto the hard bench.

"Liz, I did what you told me to." Annie's pretty face was a picture of sorrow. She dabbed at the corners of her eyes with the edge of her sleeve. "I opened myself up to Charlie, gave him a chance . . ." Her lips trembled.

Elizabeth sat down next to Annie. "And you found out what a nice guy he is, didn't you?" She eyed her friend quizzically, not comprehending the tears streaking her pink cheeks.

"Oh, Liz, I found out what a fool I've been! Just when I thought everything between us was so wonderful!" Now Annie's tears were coming more quickly than she could wipe them away. "I

don't know why I always trust people so much!"
She sniffed loudly. "I'm just dumb, I guess.
Dumb, trusting Annie. Use her and then throw
her away."

Making a giant effort to put her own unhappiness aside for a moment, Elizabeth tried to make
sense of what Annie was saying. "Who's throwing you away? Annie, take a few steps back and
start at the beginning. What happened?"

Annie glanced over toward where the tents
were set up in a sandy clearing near the road to
the campsite. She took several deep breaths,
waiting until her tears stopped before speaking.
"Well, Charlie asked me if I could pick him up
some new flashlight batteries when I was out
shopping," she began. "When I got back, I
started walking over to his tent to give them to
him. He and Bruce were inside talking. They—
they didn't see me coming. . . ." The tears began
to flow again. Elizabeth waited patiently.

"I heard my name," Annie related between
sobs. "Heard Bruce's voice. 'Annie's been with
just about every guy at Sweet Valley,' he was
saying. Just like I've heard him say so many
times before." Annie's eyes reflected the disgrace and humiliation she felt.

"Charlie stuck up for me. At least he did at
first." She made little circles in the dirt with her
toe. "I should have walked away right then, so I
wouldn't have heard the rest of it." She shook
her head wildly, as if to shake the sound of the

words she'd heard out of her mind. "Bruce kept hammering away. 'What makes you so sure people like that really change?' he asked." She paused, taking in huge gulps of air.

"And what was Charlie's reply?" Elizabeth prodded gently, almost afraid to hear Annie's answer. If misery loved company, she sensed she was about to have plenty of it.

"He said, 'Maybe you're right, Bruce.' Just like that. 'Maybe you're right.'" Annie's voice wavered on the edge of hysteria. "Maybe you're right . . ." she kept repeating. Then, as if suddenly remembering Elizabeth's presence, she stopped.

"And that was all?" Elizabeth asked.

Annie raised her shoulders in a pitiable shrug. "After that I just started to run and run, to get as far from those voices as I could." She looked Elizabeth straight in the eye. "But what am I running from, really? My own past?"

Elizabeth had no answer. She wouldn't have guessed it from Charlie. Or even from Bruce. Elizabeth had gotten the impression that his hard edge was softening as the trip progressed. But then again, maybe her judgment wasn't as sharp as she thought. Not if she'd told the only boy who mattered that she was through with him.

In a wordless gesture, she put her arms around Annie and hugged her tightly. What was there to say? The girls' grief mingled like two brooks converging in a river of overwhelming sorrow.

"Dear Enid," Elizabeth wrote:

I can now say I've been in the clamming capital of the world. It's called Pismo Beach, and for a dollar, you can bring your rake and bucket down to the shore, at low tide, and dig up all the sweet-tasting steamers you can find.

We had a great clambake right on the beach our last night there, and then it was on toward a little fishing town that turned into dune-buggy haven every afternoon. Well, you should have seen Mr. Collins churning up the sand in one of those things. He was like a professional race-car driver. He even won the weekly town race, and a feast of fresh fish for all of us as his prize.

Elizabeth concentrated on keeping her letter upbeat. There was no point in recounting a story of gloom and despair. Perhaps if Enid had actually been there, right next to her in the common room of the hostel, it would have been different. Elizabeth could have poured her feelings out to someone who always made her feel better. Lord knew she needed someone to talk to, but Jessica seemed to be having her own troubles, and Mr.

Collins was so busy trying to remain cheerful despite his problems with Ms. Dalton that Elizabeth felt it would be unfair to burden him any further.

And the other kids in the group? Elizabeth chewed on the eraser end of her pencil. By this time they'd all heard Courtney's tale of woe and were outdoing each other in their attempts to be the very nicest to her. On the other side of the common room, Courtney was engaged in a spirited game of hearts with Olivia, Roger, and Charlie.

It confused Elizabeth more than ever. Could every single one of them be wrong about Courtney? A sense of isolation weighed on Elizabeth like a cloak of lead. She had no one to turn to.

But she couldn't tell that to Enid. Her friend would just worry herself silly, when she was too far away to really do anything. No, Elizabeth had to send a cheerful letter.

She tapped her pencil against her pad of paper, then began writing again. "Then yesterday, we visited William Randolph Hearst's estate—now officially a state monument—which he called the Enchanted Hill. And I could see why."

Elizabeth launched into a description of the mansion, its Roman pool inlaid with venetian glass; the ornate gold and silver antiques; the carved woodwork; and the three stupendous guest houses.

Enid, I'd settle for one of those guest houses for my very own, with a view of the ocean and mountains, and just a smidgen of the beautiful landscape.

It's like some kind of royal palace. Of course Bruce and Lila spent the whole tour trying to outdo each other with how utterly unimpressed each one was.

Elizabeth giggled out loud. But then a scowl replaced her smile. "And Courtney had to top both of them by saying that in Beverly Hills, it would simply be another house."

Elizabeth paused and reread her last sentence. She flopped her pencil and began erasing vigorously. Any mention of Courtney was just too painful because it made her think of Todd. And under no circumstances was she going to let herself do that. She'd spent too many of the last nights crying herself to sleep, too much of the past week waiting for the trip to be over. She had to pick up the pieces of her life and forge ahead, boyfriend or no boyfriend.

She picked up her pencil again. Suddenly she hurled it to the ground. Who was she trying to fool, anyway? Enid was sure to notice that practically all Elizabeth had described were the places they'd visited. There had been no mention of Todd or of Mr. Collins and Ms. Dalton. And she'd written barely anything about anyone else on the trip, either. Enid would know immediately that something was wrong.

But what could Elizabeth tell her about her tripmates? That she hadn't seen Annie Whitman so miserable since Jessica and Cara had tried to keep her off the Sweet Valley High cheering squad? That Charlie insisted he'd stuck up for her, but Annie refused even to talk to him? That even Bruce's sincere-sounding apologies weren't enough? Or that the two trip leaders were conducting their very own cold war?

No. It just wouldn't do. Elizabeth crumpled up the sheet of notepaper and tossed it into the wastebasket next to her. She'd wait a while before writing to Enid—until things got better. She let out a long, tired sigh, sinking back on the old red-floral-print armchair in an isolated corner of the room. Things had to get better because they certainly couldn't get any worse.

But they did. First there were the arguments over where to sleep the next night. They had set out early the next morning from the hostel near the Hearst mansion, on a phantom day, before their scheduled arrival the following afternoon at Julia Pfeiffer Burns State Park in Big Sur. They'd cycled hard and covered a lot of ground, stopping later that afternoon about twenty miles south of Big Sur, to make plans.

Elizabeth got off her bicycle and stretched her long, lean legs. It felt great to relax after all that riding. In the distance the sun peeked through the clouds over the Santa Lucia mountain range, spreading rays of warm light in haphazard patches over the field where the group was gathered. Elizabeth chose one of the sunny spots and sat down, turning her face upward.

But the peace and quiet was shattered by the sound of loud voices. "I refuse to go another night without a hot shower," Lila was saying as she steered her bicycle off the road. "The nerve of that housemother, expecting us to make do with cold water!"

"Lila, it wasn't her fault that the hot-water tank was broken," Annie Whitman said in a quieter tone.

If Lila heard her, she gave no indication of it. "I absolutely insist we ride the rest of the way to Big Sur and check into the campgrounds at that state park a day early. I am *not* going to rough it again tonight."

"And *I*," Elizabeth heard her twin challenge, "refuse to ride another inch. I'm setting up a tent right here." She motioned to the wide-open, grassy plateau around them.

"You go right ahead and do that, Jessica Wakefield!" screeched Lila. "And you'll wake up by yourself. The rest of us are staying at Big Sur tonight."

Elizabeth shook her head. For two people who weren't speaking, her sister and Lila had done an awful lot of yelling and screaming at each other in the past few days. Jessica refused to tell

165

Elizabeth what the problem was, saying only that Lila wasn't worth talking to or about. Nevertheless, Jessica had seized every opportunity for a head-on confrontation. Elizabeth wouldn't have been the slightest bit surprised if neither Jessica nor Lila really cared where they slept that night but were simply jumping at another chance to play out their feud.

"Girls, girls," called Mr. Collins, parking his bicycle right next to them and making a show of covering his ears. "First of all, we're all sleeping in the same place tonight, and second, we'll decide where that is by taking a vote. Fair and square. The winner is not the one who yells the loudest."

The group was fairly evenly divided on the issue. "My sister was in Big Sur last summer," offered Charlie, "and she says it's really gorgeous. I wouldn't mind an extra night there."

"But we won't see anything tonight anyway," countered Olivia. "I mean, I'm sure it'll be dark by the time we get there."

"Not to mention that we'll be dead tired," added Annie. "I don't know about the rest of you, but I've had about enough biking today."

"Yeah, but think how terrific it'll be to get up in the morning and be there," Todd said.

"But think of all those mountains we have to ride over," Barry put in, sounding like a tape player with worn-down batteries. "I can't. I just can't."

Elizabeth's heart went out to him. Usually her motto was "Never say can't," but she was afraid that Barry was speaking the truth. "Well, if people feel they can't ride anymore," she said siding with Barry and her sister and avoiding Todd's gaze, "maybe it's not a good idea to push it."

"Well, Liz, I *can't* go without a hot shower," Lila started in again. "What do you think of that?"

Suddenly everybody seemed to be talking at once. "People! Hey, people!" Mr. Collins's voice rose over the din. "How about a show of hands?"

In the end the Big Sur faction won out, with Ms. Dalton casting the deciding vote. Elizabeth got a queasy, unsettled feeling in her stomach as the French teacher nervously looked over at Lila, met her gaze, and timidly indicated that they were of the same opinion. Elizabeth had an eerie image of Ms. Dalton as a marionette, with Lila gleefully pulling the strings. Was it another sign of something that was going wrong on this trip? Elizabeth wondered.

She rode the next twenty miles in a black cloud of gloom and despair. It wasn't so much the cycling. She was able to get up the hills at a fairly steady pace. But pushing clear of her heavy, dark thoughts was another matter.

Her preference for not going the extra distance had been purely for poor Barry's sake. Elizabeth herself didn't much care if the group stayed or

167

went. All she knew was that she wished she could be anywhere but where she was—in other words, someplace where she didn't have to see Todd and Courtney's smiling faces, hear Courtney's throaty laugh, feel that unbearable burning, aching sensation in every fiber of her body.

It was strange and awful to miss someone you saw every day, but that was how Elizabeth felt about Todd. She remembered the visit to the Hearst mansion. One room in particular had captivated her: the library, with its ornate Gothic ceilings and rare leather-bound volumes in row upon row of handsome, rich wood bookcases.

Elizabeth had imagined herself working there, turning the yellowed pages of the magnificent old books. Spellbound, she'd automatically looked around for Todd so she could share her little dream.

She caught his glance for just a moment. There had been something so sad in the depths of his brown eyes, something Elizabeth had never noticed until then. But before she could figure out if she'd imagined it or not, Courtney had sidled up next to him and whispered something in his ear. Todd had turned toward her and smiled.

Recalling the incident, Elizabeth felt the same jolt of agony rip through her as she'd felt the day it had happened. It was a torturous paradox. Todd was there, yet he wasn't. At least not for her. She could no longer watch a sunset with him by her side or tell her latest joke to him. Yet they cycled the same roads, slept in the same places, saw the same sights. His constant presence served only to make Elizabeth even more keenly aware of what she was missing.

Her own pain was coupled with Annie's and augmented by a peculiar sense of unease over Ms. Dalton's tension with Mr. Collins, and now also the way she'd reacted to Lila. Elizabeth was so lost in the overwhelming jumble of feelings inside her that she barely noticed the fact that she'd ridden the last five miles of the day's trip in a foggy darkness.

She followed the night-lights of the cyclists in front of her as they rode through the entrance to the state park and down the narrow road to the campsite.

Cheering erupted as the first members of the group parked their bicycles. "At last!" Bruce shouted, breaking out a six-pack of soda that they'd bought earlier in the day.

"Hey, Bruce! Toss one of those over here," Todd called to him.

But Elizabeth was in no mood for celebrating. Rather than put a damper on the impromptu party that was beginning, she quietly wandered off down a tiny dirt path behind the campsite. She walked slowly, her feet sinking into the muddy earth with each step. She stopped when she came to a huge fallen tree. She sat down on it

169

and stared straight ahead in the wet, black, silent fog.

She didn't know how long she sat there. Long enough to remember the first time she and Todd had ever really noticed each other, in Mr. Russo's science class, and their first kiss outside the Wakefields' front door. And all the sweet, loving times after that. And then—

"Mind if I join you?"

Elizabeth spun around, her hands gripping the rough bark of the tree trunk underneath her. "Who's there?" She squinted into a beam of light piercing the inky night.

"Liz, it's me," a soft voice said. "Barry. Did I frighten you? Look, it's no one to be afraid of. Just slow-as-molasses me." He made a weak attempt at a laugh, turning his flashlight up toward his face.

"Oh, Barry. It's OK. I wasn't scared. Maybe a little startled. I was kind of far away—you know, lost in thought and everything."

Barry sat down next to her. "Yeah, I think I do know." Sadness echoed in his words.

"Some of the kids getting you down?" Elizabeth asked gently.

Barry nodded. "So what else is new, right?"

Elizabeth gave him a sympathetic pat on the shoulder. "Don't pay any attention to them," she advised.

"I'm afraid that's impossible," Barry said dejectedly. "I've tried ignoring the comments, but how long can I keep pretending everything's fine?" He kicked at some twigs. "Besides, everything they say is true. Whatever I touch goes bad. I can't do anything right. And I'm the biggest slowpoke on two wheels."

"Barry, you know the old saying—slow and steady wins the race. Just keep on riding and doing your best. It's all anyone can possibly ask of you."

"Liz, I appreciate your being so nice to me. Believe me, it's the only thing that's kept me going sometimes. But let's face it. I'm not going to win any race. Ever. I just keep getting farther and farther behind. Like tonight, I got here at least a half hour after everybody else. How do you think it feels, always panting and pushing my bicycle way behind the others, with Mr. Collins or Ms. Dalton right on my tail, bringing up the rear? That's me—the rear."

Elizabeth listened patiently as Barry continued. "You know, I thought this trip might help me—give me a new image or something." He laughed bitterly. "But it's only making me feel worse."

"There are more terrible things than being last," Elizabeth remarked, picking at a piece of bark and thinking of her own gloomy situation.

"Yeah, like being a total klutz. Like always saying the wrong thing at the wrong time. Like making a fool out of myself over someone as popular and pretty as Jessica."

171

Elizabeth sat up as she heard her sister's name. "Barry, you're not the first boy Jessica's turned her back on. There are plenty of others. You're in good company," she joked.

Barry didn't smile. "If she'd just be my friend, I think it'd help. Maybe the others would take a cue from her. But—well, it's everything else, too. I just can't win. And this trip is no place for losers, Liz. I'm thinking maybe I should give up and go home."

"Barry! Don't even say that!" Elizabeth's words cut through the cool night air. "Just imagine how you'd feel if you quit now."

"It would be just one more thing I couldn't do," Barry said quietly.

"Barry Cooper! You *can* do it. You've come more than halfway already, so don't tell me you can't do the rest. Maybe it's been harder for you than the others, but you're here, aren't you? Do you know how many hundreds of miles you've ridden already?"

Barry nodded.

"Don't you feel kind of proud of yourself?" she continued.

"I guess. I suppose I never even really believed I could get this far."

"And how about all the beautiful places we've been to along the way? Haven't they counted for anything?"

"You've got me there, Liz. I have to admit that

most of what I'm used to in Ohio is miles and miles of cornfields."

"California is pretty spectacular," Elizabeth concurred. "And from everything I've heard, when we get a little daylight around here, we're going to see some truly amazing country. Stick around, Barry. You won't be sorry."

"You make a good case, Liz, but I don't know. I really don't know."

"Not convincing enough, huh?"

"Hey, it's not you, Liz. Everything you've said is true. It's me. When I see everyone else laughing and having fun, I feel so lonely. And I can't help it. I just want to get away."

Overhead, the wind rustled the leaves. Elizabeth couldn't argue with Barry. Because deep down, she felt exactly the same way.

Twelve

"Quick, Jess, get it!" shouted Charlie. "Get the Frisbee before it goes in the water!"

Jessica ran as fast as she could toward the spinning disk, kicking up sand and then mud, making a desperate dive for it as it disappeared into the waves. She waded into the ocean, squinting down into the white, foamy caps of water for a glimpse of yellow plastic.

"Is this what you're looking for?" a deep voice asked.

Jessica's gaze traveled upward—a pair of suntanned, muscular legs covered with fine, golden hairs, a lean, taut stomach, broad chest, a powerful pair of arms holding the Frisbee, and finally, wet curls framing a strong, handsome face, deep-set green eyes, and an amused smile. Jessica gasped.

"No, it's not Bart Templeton." Robbie October

laughed, drops of saltwater glistening on his shoulders.

Jessica simply stared. Were her eyes playing tricks on her? Or had fate given her the one lucky chance she'd been dreaming about? It couldn't have happened in a better place, either. With its misty canyons, the fierce ocean that crashed up against the mountain coast, the forests of proud, ancient redwoods, Big Sur was the perfect spot to fall in love.

"So how did your hamburgers turn out?" Robbie asked, a teasing smirk pulling at the corners of his mouth.

Jessica came down to earth with a thud. "Oh—uh—fine," she managed. Now why couldn't she, of all people, come up with something more clever to say? "Are you staying around here?" *Boring, boring, boring*, she thought.

"Yeah, over in the state park," Robbie answered, still holding the Frisbee. "It's pretty cool. No houseparents or rules to follow or anything."

"We're there, too!" Jessica said enthusiastically. "It seems nice so far."

Robbie only nodded.

"But I mean, we just got here late last night, so I don't really know what's around. What have you discovered?" Jessica kept talking. She couldn't let Robbie walk out of her life again.

"Hey, Jess! Jessica!" Charlie yelled from the

sand, over the roar of the surf. "Are you going to toss that thing, or what?"

Jessica scowled. Why did someone always come along whenever she got Robbie alone? But it wasn't the worst opportunity to show off her graceful backhand throw.

"May I?" she said to Robbie, letting her hand lightly graze his, as she took the Frisbee from him. She pushed one leg forward in the knee-deep water as she swung her arm and snapped her wrist, releasing the shiny disk in a smooth-sailing arc. "You go ahead and play without me," she called as Charlie jumped up and plucked the Frisbee out of midair. She turned back toward Robbie.

"Nice throw," he commented, his eyes tracing the curves of her lithe body, barely covered by a copper-colored bikini.

Now this is more like it, she thought, showering him with her most dazzling smile. "So. You were about to tell me all the best things to do around here." *Especially the things for two*, she added to herself.

"Well, there's some great hiking in the forest around the campgrounds. And, oh, there's this amazing waterfall that goes right down into the ocean. It's pretty wild."

"Sounds beautiful." Jessica nodded. Then, as if as an afterthought, she added casually, "Maybe you could show it to me."

Robbie's brow wrinkled. "I don't know,

Jessica. My brother and I are supposed to go windsurfing with this guy we met. He's got a car, and we're driving down the coast a ways. We might not get back until late."

"And tomorrow?" Jessica could feel her pulse speeding up nervously.

"We're leaving tomorrow."

"You are?" Jessica took an anxious step toward Robbie, foamy water swirling around her calves, as she ran her hand lightly up and down his arm. "But we're just getting to know each other!"

Robbie met her aqua-eyed glaze. "Well, I guess there's always tonight. That is, if you can tear yourself away from the rest of your group." He seemed almost to be challenging her.

"You're on!" she told him. "But we have to make it late. After everybody's asleep." *Say yes*, she wished fervently. *You've got to say yes*. Her heart was beating with excited anticipation, but she did her best to remain cool and calm. "You don't mind, do you?" she asked levelly. "I mean, I'll bet you're a night person, anyway." She arched one eyebrow suggestively.

Robbie took another careful look at her, his gaze caressing every inch of her. "You're right!" he said finally. "I am a night man."

Jessica allowed herself a triumphant grin. "Meet you at the entrance to the campgrounds at midnight?" she asked.

"OK." Robbie nodded. "If you're sure you can swing it with your group, and everything."

"Don't you worry." Jessica's voice was confident now. "I'll take care of everything."

Nora Dalton pulled herself through the water with long, even strokes, out past the breakers to where the ocean rolled gently. She flipped over on her back and let the waves rock her like a small child in its mother's arms. She made a conscious effort to relax, breathing deeply to release the tensions that overwhelmed her. It was so complex—Roger Collins, Lila, her emotions pulling her one way, the terrible secret of her past pulling her another.

She twisted back onto her stomach and took a couple of breaststrokes parallel to the shore. Under the glinting surface of the water, something caught her eye. She swam closer to investigate it.

Suddenly, a few feet away from it, she froze, letting out a terrified scream.

Roger Collins was on his feet in a flash. "Nora! Nora, are you all right?" He ran down to the water's edge.

"A—a stingray." Ms. Dalton managed, her voice hoarse as she stared with horror at the creature with its threatening, poisonous spikes and its long, spiny tail thrashing as it moved in closer.

Mr. Collins needed no coaxing. He charged into the waves, fighting the current as he raced toward Ms. Dalton. "Back away from it," he yelled, propelling himself forward with a speed he didn't know he had.

But Nora Dalton flailed her arms in panic, took one final gasp of air, and disappeared beneath the surface of the water. Roger Collins swam even faster and soon reached her side. Without a moment's hesitation he swung his left arm across her chest, holding her against him as he fought the water with his right arm and kicked with his legs. He pulled her into the shallow water, and together they stumbled onto shore.

Nora Dalton collapsed in his grasp, her head resting weakly on his shoulder. "Roger!" She wound her arms around him. "Roger, I was so frightened." She shivered, her wet body so near his. He could hear her heart pounding as she pressed her palms against the small of his back.

For the first time in months, Roger Collins was not confused. There was no anger in him, no hurt battling against his attraction and, yes, his love for Nora Dalton. He pulled her even closer. "I'm so glad you're OK. Oh, Nora, I've missed you so much."

Suddenly she pulled back like a boomerang changing direction in midflight. She was looking past him, a frightened look appearing in her large eyes.

Mr. Collins turned abruptly and followed her

stare. Farther down on the wide sand beach, the kids in the group were watching with concern.

"Are you all right, Ms. Dalton?" Elizabeth called out.

Ms. Dalton nodded yes, but her eyes never met Elizabeth's. It was hard to say for certain, but it looked to Roger Collins as if her gaze was locked on Lila Fowler. He felt Nora Dalton shrug out of his arms. "Thank you," she said in a tone that revealed nothing. She widened the space between them. "Thank you for rescuing me." Her voice was void of any emotion.

Roger Collins looked down and dug his big toe into the sand. "Yeah. Anytime," he answered. For the briefest moment, everything had been right. All his doubts over Nora Dalton had melted in her embrace. But that moment had vanished so quickly, he couldn't be sure he hadn't simply imagined it.

Lila couldn't believe her ears. Jessica Wakefield apologizing to her?

"I've been thinking about it, and I guess I overreacted," Jessica was saying. "I really am sorry." She bowed her head ever so slightly, the picture of humility.

Lila grinned. "Does that mean you're ready to be friends with Courtney?"

Jessica's brow furrowed. Having to apologize was one thing. Besides, it would be worth it in the end. But giving in to Courtney? That was taking it one step too far. "Wel-l-l, I didn't say that. But I guess I've decided that there's no reason why you shouldn't be friends with her. You're your own person, after all."

"Gee, how nice of you to allow me that," Lila said sarcastically.

Jessica affected a hurt expression, her mouth turning down, her cheeks sucked in. "Lila, you don't have to be so snooty. I mean it. I really do. And you know how hard it is for me to admit I'm wrong."

"Well *that* certainly is the truth!" Lila nodded emphatically.

"Look, Lila, it's no fun being at war with you. So let's make up, OK?"

Lila studied her friend suspiciously. "Why now, Jess?"

"Why not?" Jessica shrugged nonchalantly.

"I don't know. You tell me." Lila plucked at a blade of grass as she sat at the edge of the campsite.

"You know, Lila, you're making this really hard on me." Jessica stood up abruptly. "Maybe I should forget the whole thing." It was a calculated risk, but she had to take it. She turned on her heel and began walking away. Slowly. As slowly as she could without being obvious.

"Wait! Jessica!" She stopped as Lila called her name. A risk well taken. Jessica twisted back around.

"Don't go. I don't want us to be mad at each other either," Lila said.

Jessica ran back and threw her arms around Lila. "Friends?"

"Friends," Lila said.

"Great! It was a real drag sharing a tent with Annie last night," Jessica said. "She's been acting weird ever since she stopped speaking to Charlie."

"Yeah, well Olivia's no barrel of laughs, either. She's got her flashlight on until some ridiculous hour, scribbling poems in her little notebook all night." Lila put her hand over her heart and made herself look serious. "To my darling Roger," she recited. "You are like a drop of cream in my morning tea."

The two girls cracked up. "So you wouldn't mind getting them to change tents?" Jessica asked as their laughter died down.

Lila shook her head. "It'll be great to have you to giggle with tonight."

"You're right," Jessica agreed. *Except that tonight I don't plan on being anywhere near that tent*, she thought silently, a smile spreading across her face.

Thirteen

Lila opened one eye and looked sleepily around the tent. The weak early-morning light filtered through the green nylon. "Jess?" Lila reached out to the other side of the tent. "Jessica!" She bolted into a sitting position, her eyes wide open now. Alone! She was all alone in the tent.

She unsnapped the mesh screen at the front of the tent, lifted the nylon flap, and poked her head out. The sun, still low in the sky, was struggling to peep through a thick cloud cover. Everyone was still asleep. Jessica was nowhere in sight.

"Darn her!" Lila muttered out loud. She pulled back into the tent. Why had she let herself trust Jessica in the first place? The only reason that two-faced liar had apologized was so she could have a tentmate who wouldn't snitch on her when she sneaked off with Robbie October in the middle of the night!

183

Lila wanted nothing more than to go straight to Mr. Collins and tell him everything. But of course that was out of the question. Tattling was for goody-goodies like Olivia Davidson, or nerds like Barry Cooper, but not for people like Lila Fowler. Spreading a little gossip among friends every once in a while was one thing, but telling on someone to an adult was another story. It simply wasn't done. And besides, now Jessica owed her one—a big one. It was worth keeping her mouth shut.

But Jessica should have been back already. Where was she? Lila wondered nervously. Lost in the woods somewhere? Where was Lila supposed to draw the line between tattling and getting help for someone who might need it? "Darn!" she exclaimed again. Wasn't it just like Jessica to stick her with this kind of responsibility?

But, no. There probably wasn't anything to worry about. Knowing Jessica, she was off having a marvelous time with her precious Robbie, not giving a second thought to Lila or anyone else. Lila clenched her fists. Well, in that case, Jessica deserved to be found out. It was her problem if she didn't get back to camp before the others woke up.

"Yeah, her problem," Lila mumbled to herself, her words ending in a big yawn. She stretched out, buried her head under a pink cashmere sweater, and went back to sleep.

"Jess, Lila, c'mon! Everyone else is awake already." A couple of hours later Elizabeth's voice cut into Lila's dreams.

Lila stretched her arms and legs inside her sleeping bag. The early-morning sounds had given way to the chatter of voices, the crackle of a campfire for making breakfast, and the patter of a light drizzle hitting the sides of the tent. Lila immediately rolled over on her side and opened her eyes. Jessica's sleeping bag was still empty.

Lila was wide awake in an instant. Now what? She pulled on a pair of navy-and-white gym shorts and a matching T-shirt. Reaching into her saddlebags, she pulled out her toothbrush and a tube of toothpaste, then crawled out of the tent.

Elizabeth waited for her sister to follow Lila. "Jessica, how come you're always the last one up?" she called out.

"She's not in there," Lila said, sailing past her without stopping.

Elizabeth rushed after Lila and grabbed her arm. "Where is she?"

Lila shrugged, looking at a spot in back of Elizabeth's head. "How should I know. Look, Liz. I have to go wash up. Maybe she took a walk or something." She shrugged out of Elizabeth's grasp and headed for the facilities at the center of the campground.

"Trust Jessica to hold the rest of us up when we're trying to get out," grumbled Bruce, coming up next to Elizabeth.

"I don't know," Elizabeth responded. "It's not like her to go for an early-morning stroll. She's pretty greedy about her beauty sleep." Elizabeth tried to joke off Jessica's absence, but she felt very uneasy.

Jessica was still not back by the time Lila returned to the campsite.

"C'mon, Lila, spill it," demanded Bruce. "You must know where she went."

"Yeah, I want to get going soon," Roger agreed. "Riding in the dark with a loaded bike the other day wasn't too much fun. I don't think I'm interested in repeating the experience."

Elizabeth watched as Lila stared at the ground. "As someone once said, 'I am not my brother's keeper.' "

"But you *are* your tentmate's keeper," said Mr. Collins, joining the group that was gathering around Lila. "Do you know where Jessica is?"

"No," Lila told him in a small voice. "I don't have any idea."

"Mr. Collins, I think it'd serve Jessica right if we left without her," Bruce insisted. "That'll teach her to go off and leave us waiting."

"Bruce, did you ever stop to think that she might be in trouble somewhere?" Olivia put in. By now the whole group was assembled.

"Olivia might be right." Mr. Collins looked grim.

Elizabeth felt her alarm increasing. "Lila, are you absolutely positive you didn't hear her leave?" she asked. Lila was chewing her finger-nails nervously now.

"Lila, the woods around here can be danger-ous." Mr. Collins was gentle but firm. "Covering for a friend is one thing." He paused. "But Jessica may need our help."

"Please," Elizabeth added. She reached out and touched Lila's hand.

"I don't know how I always let her get me involved in these things." Lila pouted.

Elizabeth sighed. "Lord knows I've asked myself the same thing more times than I can count."

"Well, I'm not going to put up with it." Lila stamped her foot. "Just wait until I get a hold of her!"

Mr. Collins put his arm around Lila's shoul-der. "Lila, we have to find her first." His fore-head was etched with concern.

Lila made patterns in the sandy ground with her foot. "Well"—she hesitated—"you know that guy, Robbie October?"

"You mean the one she was talking to on the beach yesterday?" Elizabeth asked.

Lila nodded.

"What about him?" Elizabeth coaxed.

"She went off to meet him someplace," Lila answered. "I think they were going for a hike back in those woods." She made a vague gesture at the forest looming up behind her.

"First thing in the morning?" Ms. Dalton seemed puzzled.

Lila lowered her head, her light-brown hair falling over her face. Elizabeth had to strain to hear her words. "Not this morning," she admitted miserably. "Last night. She left after everyone went to bed."

Elizabeth gasped. "Omigod! I've got to find her!" She dashed over to her tent, grabbed her tennis shoes, and frantically pulled them over her bare feet. She could feel the adrenaline speeding through her body.

"Now wait a minute, Liz." Mr. Collins put a hand on her shoulder. "You can't go rushing off by yourself in those woods. They're enormous. You couldn't begin to know where to look for Jessica. Pretty soon, you'd be lost, too."

"Mr. Collins, I *can't* just sit here, knowing my sister might need me!" Her voice rose, out of control.

"I'm not suggesting we sit around doing nothing." Mr. Collins's voice was soothing. "But we have to be organized about it. One person missing is more than enough. Now, Lila, are you sure Jessica didn't say anything else about where she was going? Think hard," he encouraged. "It could be crucial."

Lila shook her head. "All she said was that she was meeting him at the gate to the campgrounds." Lila bit her lip. "Oh, wait!" She looked up suddenly. "And something about a waterfall."

"Of course!" Todd snapped his fingers. "It's off one of the park's hiking trails. I went up there yesterday when you were all at the beach. It's really beautiful."

"OK, then," Mr. Collins said decisively. "You go with Liz and show her the way."

Elizabeth and Todd looked at each other uncomfortably. "Well, actually, there are two different trails that connect up before the waterfall—" Todd began.

But in the frenzy over Jessica, Mr. Collins missed the point of Todd's remark. "Then you two take the first one. I'll take another group in the second direction."

Elizabeth simply nodded. This was no time for protests or explanations.

"The rest of you wait here," Mr. Collins continued. "If Jessica returns before we do, send a third party out to get us. If we're not back in an hour, go for the park rangers. Todd, I want you to make a sketch here of where those trails begin." The trip leader took a felt-tipped pen out of his pocket and tore a section of brown paper from a grocery bag.

Todd made a hasty drawing, looking up in the middle to meet Elizabeth's nervous glance. "We'll find her," he said quietly. "Don't worry." They were the first words he had spoken to her since that fateful morning. It was only a few days earlier, but those days had moved so slowly Elizabeth felt as if months had gone by since the last time she'd been in Todd's tender embrace.

Now, hearing his voice so gently reassuring her, Elizabeth felt tears well up in her blue-green eyes. It was all too much—Jessica, Todd, Courtney . . .

As if reading her thoughts, Courtney stepped over and put a hand on Elizabeth's back. "Please don't cry," she said.

Elizabeth spun to face the other girl. Was it her imagination, or was there a hard look in Courtney's eye that didn't go at all with her syrupy sweet tone?

But Courtney continued, her voice oozing sympathy. "Jessica will be fine. I'll even come help find her."

Elizabeth shuddered. Courtney was as transparent as a newly washed window. She didn't care a fig about Jessica. Why couldn't anyone else see that?

"That's so nice of you. We could use the help." Now Todd's quiet words were for Courtney.

Elizabeth felt a flush of anger rise to her cheeks. But there was no time for arguing or for explaining the whole sticky situation to Mr. Collins. Jessica had to come first.

Elizabeth nodded glumly at Todd and Courtney. "The sooner we get started, the better," she said.

* * *

"It's all my fault!" Lila paced back and forth like a caged animal. "I shouldn't have let her go. Then none of this would have happened!"

Almost a half hour had gone by, and neither of the search parties had returned. Charlie and Roger had volunteered to go in Mr. Collins's group, and Barry had insisted on joining them.

"It could be a very strenuous walk." Mr. Collins had dropped a tactful hint to Barry. "And we're going to be moving as quickly as possible."

But Barry, as worried over Jessica as Elizabeth herself had been, refused to stay behind. "I want to help find her," he'd announced.

But even someone as slow as Barry Cooper should have been able to make it to the waterfall and back by now, thought Lila. "If I were any kind of a real friend, I would have been worried about her, instead of rolling over and going back to sleep," she mumbled to herself.

"You're darned right, Fowler," Bruce said, poking at the ashes of the past night's fire with a twig. "We ought to be halfway to Monterey by now." Lila didn't bother to answer. Even Bruce sounded more worried than anything else.

But sitting on the picnic table, her legs dangling over the side, Annie shook her head vehemently. "Bruce, don't you think she feels bad enough already?"

Bruce turned and fixed Annie with a scowl.

191

"And you, Annie. You treat me like, I don't know, one of these pieces of wood." He stabbed at a burned log from the campfire. "You know, I'll admit that I haven't always acted like a friend to you, but lately I've really been trying. And you make me feel like I'm no better than a—a—"

"Tramp?" finished Annie. "That's your favorite word, isn't it—or at least it's what you call me." She hopped off the table and went over to Bruce, crouching in front of him. "You might as well say the word to my face because you certainly haven't been shy about saying it behind my back!"

Bruce frowned, running a hand through his dark, thick hair, damp from the intermittent rain. "I don't think you're being fair, Annie. All that happened ages ago."

"Ages ago? Try a few days ago. I know what you and Charlie said in your tent." Annie recounted the conversation she had overheard, her anger dissolving into anguish as she echoed Charlie's words.

Understanding registered in Bruce's blue eyes. "Annie, you should have stuck around for the rest of the conversation." His tone was softer now. "What Charlie actually said to me was 'Maybe you're right, Bruce, *but I don't think so!*' Annie, he really cares about you. He even convinced me to give you a chance . . ."

Annie's expression was slowly changing, her brow relaxing, her lips turning upward.

". . . and I'm pretty tough to convince, if I say so myself!" Bruce continued.

"You mean to say," began Annie, "that all this time? . . ." Her voice trailed off as the realization hit home.

Bruce nodded.

Annie's smile was full-fledged now. "Bruce Patman, if I didn't know better, I'd swear you were turning into a softie."

Bruce smiled back and put a finger over his lips. "But let's keep it between us, OK? After all, I have a reputation to uphold!"

Elizabeth's tennis shoes were caked with mud. The rain was coming down harder now, and her hair fell in wet strands around her shoulders. They were nearing the point where they were supposed to rendezvous with Mr. Collins's group, and there was still no trace of Jessica.

"Jess! Jessica Wakefield!" Elizabeth called, her voice hoarse from shouting the same desperate refrain over and over. She led Todd and Courtney out of the forest of redwoods into a marshy clearing.

Suddenly, behind her Courtney let out a piercing shriek. Elizabeth spun around. "Oh, my God! A snake! Help, Todd!" Courtney had her arms stretched out in front of her as if to push away the horrid vision.

Todd stepped forward. "Courtney, it's only a harmless little water snake."

Courtney didn't budge. "Look, it's pouring, we're soaked to the bone, we haven't found the first clue about Jessica, and there are horrible things slithering all around. And on top of all that, I'm getting a terrible cold. I think we should turn around and go back." She let out a well-timed sneeze.

Elizabeth tried to be sympathetic, but no matter how she looked at it, all she could see was the old Courtney, fighting her way through all the new sweetness.

The small black snake slithered away and disappeared under a rock. "What about Jessica?" Todd gave Courtney a funny look. "You do care about her, don't you?"

Courtney moved closer to him and linked her arm through his. Elizabeth felt every cold, aching muscle in her body tense up. "Of course I do, Todd." The new Courtney was back in control, gazing up at him as innocent as a newborn lamb. "I just think maybe we should let a professional do it. I mean, the park rangers *are* trained to find people." She sneezed again.

Elizabeth slapped at a mosquito on her arm. "You two can do whatever you want. I'm not giving up." There was a fierceness in her voice that sounded strange, even to her own ears.

"Nobody said anything about giving up," said Todd. "But if Courtney's getting sick, we ought

194

to get her back to camp right away. We don't want to create any more problems than we already have."

Courtney looked from Todd to Elizabeth. The tension was so thick, Elizabeth felt she could almost cut it with a knife. She felt as if they were life-size pieces in a crucial game of chess. Now it was Courtney's move.

She sniffled dramatically. "Listen, I can find my own way back. You two keep looking for Jessica. She's more important than I am right now, anyway." It was a move, Elizabeth decided, that was perfectly calculated to go straight to Todd's heart.

Todd responded right on cue. "No, Courtney, you can't wander around here by yourself. Especially if you're not feeling well."

Elizabeth wished the earth would open up and swallow her. At that second, it seemed as though nothing would ever go right for her again.

The long, excruciating silence was pierced by voices calling Jessica's name. "There's the other group," Elizabeth said abruptly. "I'll go with them. Todd, you can take Courtney back to the campgrounds." Her tone was tight as she willed herself not to shed a tear.

Todd nodded wearily. "I guess that's the best solution."

"I guess," Elizabeth echoed, with fire in her words. She turned on her heel and started walk-

195

ing. She looked back only once. Courtney was already headed in the other direction, but Todd was standing right where Elizabeth had left him, looking at her. Elizabeth steeled herself and turned back around. She couldn't let herself soften toward Todd. His decision was clear. It had been ever since the night in the greenhouse. Courtney was the girl he'd chosen.

Fourteen

It was a standoff: Jessica and Robbie against the stocky black bear.

"Robbie, when we get out of this cave, I never want to see you again." Even at a whisper, the fear and anger in Jessica's voice came across strong and clear. "This whole thing is your fault!"

"I don't see how you figure that," Robbie hissed back. "You were the one who was so keen on coming up here in the middle of the night!"

Jessica and Robbie were huddled behind a large rock. Every time either of them moved too suddenly or spoke too loudly, the bear would let loose a ferocious roar and lumber a step or two closer to them.

"How was I supposed to know you were dumb enough to go out without a flashlight and get us totally lost before we even got to that waterfall? I don't know how you expected us to see it, anyway." Jessica's teeth chattered as she pulled her damp sweater closer around her.

"I didn't get the feeling," retorted Robbie, "that the fun you had in mind depended on seeing anything at all."

Fun! Ha! thought Jessica. It had turned out to be one of the most miserable nights of her life, lying cold and exhausted under a giant redwood, waiting until it got light enough to figure out where they were. Every time her eyes had closed and she'd begun falling asleep, snapping branches, falling leaves, or the call of some wild night bird would remind her that she was in hostile territory with a hundred and one varieties of creepy, crawly creatures all around her.

When the first rays of the sun had warmed the distant mountaintops, Jessica had assumed her twisted misadventure was almost over.

Wrong! The worst was yet to come, in the form of a cloudburst that sent her and Robbie running to a nearby cave for shelter from the rain. They hadn't noticed the two bear cubs sleeping on a ledge near the front of the cave until the mother bear had returned from gathering food for her babies. By then, it was too late. And although they had hidden behind the large rock, they were trapped inside the cave!

"Well at least she's not one of those killer bears you read about," Robbie whispered after a long silence. "I mean she doesn't seem to want to bother us. You know she probably could come over here and really mess us up, if she wanted to."

"Robbie, you have such a way with words," Jessica replied snidely.

"Look, Jess. I'm just trying to say we're lucky we're still alive."

Jessica fixed Robbie with an icy glare. "I don't feel so lucky. For all I know, we could starve to death before we get out of here. And worst of all, I'd be going to my grave with *you*, of all people." Jessica's voice flared heatedly.

At the mouth of the cave, the mother bear snarled out a warning. "Sshhh," Robbie ordered harshly. "If you don't keep your voice down, you're not even going to get a chance to starve to death."

Sitting on the hard, damp cave floor, Jessica dropped her face into her hands. She knew her verbal sparring with Robbie was really a cover-up for her terror. It was a no-win situation. If they moved from behind the rock, the bear might attack; if they didn't there was no possibility of escaping. She let out a low moan of fear.

"Scared, Jessica?" Robbie said. "Some big, tough adventurer you turned out to be. Maybe next time you'll stick to burning hamburgers."

Jessica didn't answer. She sensed that behind his disdain, Robbie was just as frightened as she was.

"Jessica? Jess?" At first Jessica thought she

was imagining it—a voice outside the cave, calling from a distance. Barry Cooper's voice!

Jessica lifted her face up, ready to yell for help, when Robbie's arm shot out and he slapped his palm over her mouth. "Don't you dare!" His voice trembled. "One good scream, and she'll probably charge."

Jessica peeled Robbie's hand away from her face. "If you're so brave, what's your bright idea? Or are we just going to sit here and hope? If we don't take any chances, we'll never get rescued." Before Robbie could stop her, she half stood and gave an ear-piercing shriek. "Barry! In here!"

The bear lunged forward. Jessica crouched behind the rock again. She could hear the bear's paws pounding against the cave floor. Closer. The ground shook.

Suddenly the bear stopped. Jessica peeked out around the rock. The bear was no more than two feet away. Jessica didn't dare even breathe.

"Jessica, is that you? Where are you?" Barry's voice rang out more strongly. The bear turned and lumbered toward that sound.

"Barry! Get help! A bear—" Jessica screamed. "Her cubs are in here with us." The bear spun back around.

"Don't panic, Jessica," Barry shouted back. The bear looked out of the cave again. Barry could see her now, squat and heavy, her fur a shiny black, with yellowish highlights around the chest and stomach. She growled as she reared up, turning from Barry to her captives in the cave and then back again.

"I'll get the others," Barry yelled as loudly as he could. The bear took a step or two toward him.

Barry began to run, looking over his shoulder as he moved. The bear stayed where she was. "Mr. Collins, Liz—I've found her!" Barry called out. His voice bounced off the massive redwood columns that surrounded him. He pumped his legs until he could feel them burn. Faster, faster he pushed himself. How far had he lagged behind? He could only hope against hope that the rest of the group wasn't too far away. He heaved and panted, the forest a blur as he pressed forward.

Jessica. Jessica. His footsteps seemed to echo her name. His throat stung. He stumbled. He had to keep going. Up ahead he heard voices. "Mr. Collins, Charlie. I've found her. I've found Jessica. Roger, Liz, everyone hurry."

Elizabeth was the first to reach Barry, who was doubled over and taking in huge gulps of air. "Where? Barry, which way?"

Barry took a few more deep breaths and was back on his feet. Elizabeth followed him to the cave, the three others were close behind. "Is Jessica OK?" She tugged at the sleeve of Barry's sweater.

Her answer was the ear-shattering roar of a

bear. Elizabeth screamed. The bear faced her and roared again. "Jess!" she shouted.

"Liz! Oh, my God! Help!" Jessica replied, panic-stricken. The bear turned round and round in a confused circle, growling first at the rescue party, then at her prisoners in the cave.

"She's getting confused," Mr. Collins said edgily. "And it isn't making her any friendlier."

"Should we call the police?" Roger Patman suggested.

"No time." Mr. Collins didn't mince words. "Who knows what that bear might do while we're waiting for someone to arrive."

Charlie picked up a rock and pulled his arm back over his head. "There's only one thing to do," he announced grimly.

But before he could fling his arm forward again and release the stone, Barry reached up and seized his arm. "No!" he said forcefully.

Elizabeth's mouth dropped open in shock. She'd never seen Barry so assertive.

"What do you mean, no?" Charlie's own astonishment rang through the air. "If we don't get that thing first, it's going to get Jessica. We don't have any other choice."

"Charlie, that thing is a living creature, a mother trying to protect her babies. She thinks we want to hurt them."

Charlie looked down at Barry, still clutching the stone. "You picked a heck of a time to reveal the animal lover in you, buddy. But let me remind you of all those stories about campers getting mauled by bears."

"Not these bears." There was a tone of authority in Barry's words, a certainty that made Elizabeth want to pinch herself to make sure she wasn't dreaming. Was this the same helpless Barry who'd been the butt of so many jokes?

"She's a black bear," Barry continued. "Usually they live farther north than this, but there are a few around here. And she's one of them. They're not violent. At least not unless you confront them."

Elizabeth and Mr. Collins exchanged a look of total astonishment. Who would have guessed that under his insecure, butter-fingered pudgy exterior, Barry was an expert on animals? No one knew. No one had bothered to find out.

"Listen, Barry, I don't see how we can get Jessica out of there *without* a confrontation, do you?" Charlie asked.

Barry appeared stuck for an answer. Suddenly everything was happening at once. The bear growled fiercely again. From inside the cave, Jessica pleaded for help. "She's getting crazier by the second. Somebody, do something." Charlie lifted his arm once more.

"Oh, please! Help us!" Now Robbie's screams mingled with Jessica's. Charlie took aim.

"Charlie, don't!" Barry ran right in front of Charlie and didn't stop until he was inches from the bear. He swatted out at her, almost touching her.

"Barry!" Elizabeth cried in panic.

The bear opened her mouth and lurched at Barry. He jumped out of the way. She went at him again, and Barry started running, the bear in pursuit. The mouth of the cave was clear at last, and Jessica and Robbie came flying out, Jessica heading straight for Elizabeth's arms.

The bear was still lumbering after Barry. She was fast for so bulky a creature, reaching out with her front paws and nearly grazing Barry's back. And Barry, despite his heroic gesture, was as slow as ever. The bear was gaining on him.

Charlie moved his throwing arm as they ran, aiming and re-aiming. "It's no use. The bear's too close. If I throw this, I might hit Barry."

Elizabeth watched, helpless, petrified, as Barry lost speed. "Oh, Barry, keep going," she pleaded urgently.

And then, from deep inside the cave, came a peculiar noise. The bear stopped, and Barry scampered out of her reach. She turned around and doubled back on her tracks.

"It's one of the cubs—crying!" Elizabeth's realization filled her with joy and relief.

No one wasted a second. Roger Collins raced over to Barry, scooped the exhausted boy up, and hoisted him over his shoulder. In almost no time at all, the entire group was a good distance away from the cave. Jessica and Robbie were safe.

Elizabeth sighed with relief and thankfulness as her twin threw her arms around Barry and gave him a loud kiss on the cheek. He turned a deep shade of scarlet. Jessica kissed the other cheek. Barry's embarrassment was overshadowed only by a blissful, almost drunken smile that spread from one side of his round face to the other.

There was no doubt about it. In the space of one morning, Barry Cooper had graduated from nerd to hero.

"And there I was, thinking you agreed with Bruce." Annie's big brown eyes were moist as she gazed up at Charlie.

"When all that time, Bruce was agreeing to agree with me!" Charlie said lightly. "Don't be so hard on yourself, Annie. People make mistakes." Then his expression became serious. "I'm just glad you found out the real story." He traced her cheekbones with his fingertips, his hand coming to rest so that his palm was cupping her face.

"You mean you're not mad?" Annie studied him. His hazel eyes fringed with long lashes, his upturned nose with a smattering of freckles across the bridge, his curly, flaxen blond hair. Behind him, the Monterey harbor rose out of the bay, weatherbeaten wood shacks and board-walks perched on stilts. Behind that, the foothills of the Santa Lucia mountain range reflected the muted colors of a waning afternoon sun. "If I had only listened to your explanation right off, this whole misunderstanding wouldn't have happened."

"I must admit, for a while there I was sure you'd never speak to me again," Charlie said.

"It was really dumb of me." Annie belittled herself. "Really stupid. That's me."

"Hey, hey!" Charlie affected a tone of mock hurt. "That's one of my favorite people you're talking about!"

"It is? I mean, I am?" Annie pushed a way-ward wisp of curly dark hair out of her eyes.

Wordlessly, Charlie pulled her toward him, and their lips met. Annie felt as if a warm, golden light was coursing through her body. Their lips parted just for an instant, before coming together again. It was the only answer she needed.

"Another marshmallow, Barry?" Jessica asked sweetly. The bonfire blazed on the Monterey beach, and the bay water looked as smooth and tranquil as a lake. She pushed a marshmallow onto the end of a thin stick and twirled it slowly over the orange flames.

"Thanks, Jess," Barry said, clearly overcome

by his new status as a man of mettle. He had been just as far behind on that day's ride as always, but suddenly it wasn't the joke of the season. Suddenly he had encouragement and support and a dozen new friends. Especially Jessica. "You really don't have to," he said, as she held the golden toasted sweet out to him like an offering.

"I know," Jessica replied matter-of-factly. "So just enjoy it while it lasts." She gave a playful wink, and Barry giggled nervously. It was so easy to satisfy some people, Jessica thought. Just a smile and a couple of nice words did the trick.

Lila, on the other hand, was harder to please. She was making a big show of palling it up with Courtney on the other side of the camp fire, but every few minutes she would dart an icy glare in Jessica's direction.

"Barry, will you excuse me?" Jessica asked, getting up and brushing some sand off her black Levis. "I've got some unfinished business to take care of."

As she moved around the bonfire, she could feel Lila watching her out of the corner of her eye. "Lila, can we talk?" She stood before her friend, her hands on her hips.

"I'm all ears," Lila responded curtly.

"How about if we take a walk or something," Jessica suggested. "Because one pair of ears is enough." She directed her scowl at Courtney.

"Why, Jessica," Lila began, in a tone of mock

innocence. "Whatever do you mean? We're all friends here."

"I don't know, Lila. You don't seem all that enthusiastic about me these days. And frankly, I'm hurt." She stuck out her bottom lip in a perfect imitation of the loyal friend, unfairly wronged.

"I don't know why you say that, Jess. I like you just fine." Lila continued to play her coy game.

"Well, if you like me just fine, I don't see why you'd object to taking a walk down the beach with me."

"Oh." Lila's face grew dark, and Jessica knew her special brand of circular logic was having its effect.

"Besides," she added for insurance, "I vant to be ah-lone vit you." She pulled her sweater across the bottom of her face like a vampire's cloak and arched one eyebrow.

The corner of Lila's mouth twitched as she struggled to keep a straight face. "Oh, all right."

Jessica grinned as she grabbed Lila's hand and pulled her up. "I knew you couldn't resist me for long."

"This had better be a good one, Wakefield," Lila said as Jessica led her away from the crackling fire.

"Lila, I just wanted to tell you that I meant it the other night when I said I wanted to be friends."

"Oh, sure. And it had nothing whatsoever to do with your wanting to sneak out and meet Mr. Wonderful."

"Don't even remind me." Jessica picked up a smooth, flat pebble and spun it toward the bay. She watched it skip three times before sinking into the glittering water. "What a creep that guy turned out to be. Do you know that after he got us lost, he had the nerve to try to get romantic with me? Ugh. While I was busy at the impossible job of trying to get some sleep with all those bugs and animals and things all over the place."

"But, Jess, you were aching for Robbie to get romantic." Lila breathed a sigh of exasperation. "And besides, you're avoiding the issue."

"I only wanted him before I knew what a bumbling idiot he was. It was *his* fault I had to spend the whole night in the woods and *his* fault that I almost got eaten by a bear. I should have stayed back in the tent with you."

"Don't you think it's a little late for regrets?" Lila challenged. "While everyone was getting hysterical about you, they were yelling at me for letting you go off. It's typical. You mess up, and someone else gets in trouble."

"Well, I really am sorry, Lila. I would've had more fun with you than with Robbie. I apologize."

"I've heard that before."

"No, I mean it this time." Jessica's words were sincere. With Robbie out of the picture, she

209

really did miss Lila. When it came to giggling and gossiping, Lila was a blue-ribbon champ.

"Is that to say you didn't mean it last time?" Lila was still on edge.

"Oh, come on, Lila. Give me a break. It just means I want us to be like we were at the beginning of the trip."

Lila was silent.

" 'Fess up, Fowler. You must have been just a teeny-weeny bit worried when you realized your old friend was missing."

Lila picked at a loose stitch on her handknit Irish wool sweater. "OK, so maybe I was a little scared for you," she muttered.

"What was that, Lila? I couldn't hear you." Jessica reached out and began tickling Lila under the chin. Lila tried to get away, but Jessica was too quick. With her free hand, she grabbed her friend's arm.

"Stop! Jess! Oh, don't. You know how ticklish I am." Lila squealed for mercy.

"Then tell me how worried you were."

"All right, already. I was really scared."

Jessica let go. "I knew it! I knew you were worried sick about me!" She laughed loudly.

Lila joined in. "It's true. I was." Her tone grew serious again. "You know if anything had happened to you, I would have blamed myself."

"Thanks, Lila. You're a pal. Really."

"But this doesn't mean I'm going to leave

210

Courtney by the side of the road, so to speak," Lila warned.

"Well, I guess I can handle that," Jessica conceded. "Only you have to swear that *I'm* the friend who really counts."

"I'll give you that," Lila agreed. She moved away from the water and sat down cross-legged. Jessica followed her. "I mean you and I go back a long time. There are definitely certain things I could talk to you about that wouldn't much matter to Courtney."

"Such as?" Jessica rubbed her palms together in anticipation of the newest delectable morsel of gossip. It really *was* nice to have Lila back on her team.

"On a scale of one to ten, this one's a ten, Jess," Lila said enticingly.

"Yeah?" Jessica felt like a kid on Christmas morning, about to open the biggest present under the tree.

"But there's an advantage to keeping it a secret," Lila went on, clearly relishing her control over the conversation. "It gives me—well—a kind of power over a certain someone on this trip."

"Ms. Dalton!" Jessica said breathily.

Lila nodded gleefully.

"But you're going to tell me anyway, right?" Jessica continued. "Poor Lila, with a secret so huge bottled up inside her that she makes up with horrible, wicked Jessica Wakefield just so she'll have someone to spill the beans to."

"It's true. I can't wait to see your face when I tell you! But I *could* manage to keep it to myself, if I absolutely had to." Lila let her voice linger suggestively on her last words.

"OK, Lila. Name your price."

"Dish duty for the rest of the trip." Lila folded her arms triumphantly.

"Be serious, Lila." Jessica was indignant.

"Then you won't find out." Lila shrugged. "It's only the hottest news this side of the Rockies. Big enough to rip Ms. Dalton's career at Sweet Valley High to shreds."

"I don't know, Lila. That's an awful lot of dishes." Jessica knew her friend was ready to explode with this latest tidbit and was certain she could get the price down.

"Jessica, she's not really Nora Dalton."

Jessica let out a loud gasp. "What?!!" Her exclamation echoed over the still water.

"And that's only the beginning," Lila said.

"One week of dishes," Jessica offered. "Take it or leave it."

"It's a deal." Lila nodded. "So—are you ready for this? Her real name is Beth Curtis. I met this guy at the last hostel we stayed at, who comes from her hometown. She taught French at the high school there, too.

"So anyway, Beth Curtis comes from this little town in Arizona. She was married to a guy named John Curtis. John Mayfield Curtis the Third, to be exact, from the richest, most important family in that town. Well, Beth Curtis left John Curtis. A few days later, he killed himself."

"Oh, my God." Jessica's voice was low. She had expected some good, fun gossip. She hadn't bargained for anything this heavy. No wonder Lila needed to talk to someone about it.

Lila nodded her head. "It's true. John Curtis's family said she drove him to it. And you know what else? She didn't even go to the funeral. And she disappeared a few days later. No one knew where she went. But they all figured there was someone else involved."

Jessica felt as if a house had just fallen on her. She was stunned, speechless. Ms. Dalton was so gentle, so mild-mannered. I didn't seem possible.

"I know. I know. You don't believe it." Lila resumed talking. "You think she's the sweet type. But I told you that you didn't know her like I do. Sometimes it's those seemingly good ones who turn out to be rotten to the core. Remember Dr. Jekyll and Mr. Hyde?"

"Lila, Jekyll and Hyde are characters in a book. Ms. Dalton's a real live person." Jessica looked down the beach toward the bonfire, where she could just make out Ms. Dalton's silhouette.

"Jess, you know what I'm saying. Those nice-as-they-come people are the ones you have to watch out for."

"Maybe you're right." Jessica shook her head. "I can't decide what to think."

"I know I'm right!" Lila said with certainty. "And you know what else? I think she married John Curtis for his money. And when she got tired of him, she simply threw him away. Started up with some other man.

"She thinks she's going to do the same thing with my father." Lila grew fierce. "But now that I know the truth, I'm going to stop her. I'm going to get that woman out of my life once and for all! When I told her I knew her real identity, she begged me not to say anything. And it was sort of fun for a while, getting her to do anything I wanted just by looking at her. But, boy, soon I'm going to have my moment when I expose her to the world. So much for her plans for my father's money! No wonder Mr. Collins doesn't want to have anything to do with her anymore."

"Wait a minute, Lila. I don't know if I agree with you there," said Jessica. "From that incident at the beach the other day with the stingray, I'd say Mr. Collins is still pretty crazy about her. I think he's holding back just because she is. In fact, their whole fight doesn't make any sense, if you ask me."

"Well, it makes perfect sense to me." Lila was adamant. "That woman is dangerous, with a capital D. Mr. Collins is a smart guy. I'll bet he sees right through her."

Jessica wasn't sure. Not about Mr. Collins, nor

214

about the pretty French teacher, either. But one thing was certain. With Lila at the helm, it was going to be a rough ride for Ms. Dalton—or Ms. Curtis or whoever she really was—a horribly rough ride.

Fifteen

The coast was clear. Courtney had watched Elizabeth carefully extinguish the last smoldering embers of the camp fire with sand, until not one glowing speck remained. After what seemed like forever, Elizabeth had turned her back on the camp fire and disappeared inside her tent. In the moonlight Courtney could see that the Santa Cruz campsite was deserted.

Courtney pushed open the tent flap she'd been peering out of and made her way out of the tent, careful not to wake Ms. Dalton. The trip leader had gone to bed early with a headache—certainly no surprise, considering the rumors that were flying around about her. She didn't stir as Courtney emerged into the fresh night air.

It was getting cooler as they rode north, and she pulled her denim jacket on as she crept toward Todd's tent. "Todd. Todd," she whispered, bending close to the entrance to his tent.

Roger Patman's sleepy-looking face popped out of the flap. "Who's there?" He rubbed his eyes.

Courtney clapped her hand to her mouth. "Oh, Roger. Oh, I'm so sorry to wake you up." She poured on the sugarcoated apologies. It was such an easy game to play.

"Oh, Courtney." Roger smiled and tried to stifle a yawn. "What's up?"

"Roger, I didn't mean to bother you, but I have to talk to Todd. It's really important." She uttered her last sentence with dramatic urgency.

"What's going on?" Todd said, poking his head out of the tent. Roger drew back inside.

"Todd, I must talk to you."

"Right now? Courtney, it's the middle of the night!"

"Please. It's about Daddy." Courtney's look of worry could have won her an Oscar.

Todd's face took on an instant expression of concern. "In that case, I'll be right out. I just have to throw some clothes on."

Courtney nodded. "I'll be waiting over there." She motioned to a clearing several yards from the tents.

As she rose and walked away, she fished around in the pocket of her jacket, until her fingers found a pack of Marlboros. She tapped the red-and-white box against the side of her hand, taking a cigarette out and lighting it. It was time

217

for the final step in her plan. There was no way for it to fail now.

She inhaled deeply on the cigarette, then breathed out a thin, steady stream of smoke. Elizabeth was out, and she was in. Todd had as good as proved it the previous morning, when he'd chosen to accompany her back to the campsite.

She'd called her father. With Todd in the picture, he'd agreed to let her come home. It had taken all her best efforts in the wheedling and coaxing department, but in the end, Steve Thomas had been won over. Courtney had told him how much she missed him. And her own room. And that she'd tried, she really had, but that she just wasn't the wood-chopping, tent-pitching type.

Most of all, however, Steve Thomas had been won over because, to him, Todd Wilkins was the epitome of good, clean fun. Courtney sneered. What could be more boring? But for now, Todd was her ticket back to Beverly Hills. She was going to treat him as specially as if he were Nolan Ruggers himself.

"Courtney?" Todd was coming toward her now, tying up a pair of navy sweat pants that were topped by a white sweat shirt, with the words, SWEET VALLEY HIGH in red block letters forming an arc across his chest.

Courtney took one final puff on her cigarette and carelessly flicked the rest of it into the bushes behind her. She moved toward Todd, contorting her face into an expression of fear and anguish.

"What's wrong? Something's happened, hasn't it?" Todd's arms were around her in an instant.

Courtney made the most of this, leaning her head against Todd's broad chest and letting her fingers trail up and down his arm. "Oh, Todd, I'm so worried about Daddy," she said mournfully, punctuating her declaration with a little sob. "Every time I call him, he just sounds worse and worse."

Todd wound his arms around Courtney's back, pulling her even closer as she continued speaking. "I can just picture him in his study, pouring himself glass after glass of scotch." Her voice cracked, and she sniffled loudly.

"Shh, Courtney. Try to calm down. It's not going to help, all your worrying. You're here, and your father is there."

"I know. That's the whole problem. How am I supposed to have fun when I know he's drinking himself into oblivion? I can't stand it! I have to go home and be with him!"

"Are you saying you want to leave the trip?" Todd asked, never letting go of her.

Courtney nodded, her cheek rubbing against Todd's sweat shirt. "Everyone in this group has been so wonderful, but I can't really enjoy them, or anything else, knowing what Daddy's doing."

"You're really devoted to him, aren't you?" Todd was clearly touched.

Courtney took a deep breath. "He's the only family I have. I have to take care of him. Todd, I'm going back to him. Tomorrow. I know right now he doesn't think he wants me there, but I'm going anyway. He'll thank me for it one day."

"Then your mind is made up?" Todd asked.

"Yes. There's only one thing."

"What's that?"

Courtney pulled back slightly so she was looking at Todd. "I'm scared. It's so hard being alone with him in that house. Sometimes he just passes out in his reclining chair, but other times"—she looked grim—"he gets so wild, he could end up doing just about anything. Todd, I'm going to ask you a huge favor."

"I'll do anything I can to help." Todd reached for her hand and squeezed it tightly.

"I want to know if you'll come home with me." Courtney felt Todd shiver. Was it the cool night air, or had she gone a step too far? She did some calculated backtracking. "But I understand if you don't want to. You have Elizabeth here . . ."

Todd's brown eyes took on a sad, faraway look. "No. No, I don't. Not really. She's changed. She used to be so kind and caring. She would never have turned her back on someone who needed her. She had all the qualities that are so important to me. All the qualities—" Todd stopped in midsentence and focused on Courtney.

"Yes?" Courtney prodded.

"She had all the qualities that you have. Yes, that's it. The old Liz would have been your friend, Courtney."

"Then it's true. She really doesn't like me." Courtney made her eyes big and sorrowful.

"I'm afraid she doesn't like me much either these days."

"Poor Todd," Courtney consoled, playing her role as a good, comforting friend.

"Hey, don't worry about me." Todd made a concerted effort to toughen up. His jaw became tense with determination. "You're the one who really needs the attention."

"And so? . . ." Courtney asked. She knew it was almost in the bag.

"And so I'll come with you." Todd nodded, affirming his own decision.

"You won't be sorry," Courtney purred. "You'll be helping Daddy and me, and besides, Hollywood can be a pretty exciting place. Who knows? Maybe you'll even get to work on a movie or two." She knew Todd was up on all the latest films. It couldn't hurt to give him a little more incentive for accompanying her home.

"You think so?" Todd's voice grew brighter, and she knew she'd scored points.

"I'm sure I can arrange it." *It'll be perfect*, she thought. *That'll mean more time for Nolan and me*. She drew Todd toward her until their mouths met, the final bit of insurance that her plan was a success.

She closed her eyes and pretended it was Nolan she was kissing. Soon she wouldn't have to pretend any more. Nolan would be hers again. Thanks to Todd. In a way it was too bad. In fact, he was a pretty decent kisser. But Courtney wasn't the type for regrets. She pressed her lips against Todd's again, then drew away. "So it's set. I'll pack up my things, and we can leave first thing tomorrow."

Something was burning. Elizabeth bolted upright and was out of her tent in the blink of an eye. The grass behind the camp fire was charred, and from the bushes in back came flames and billowing, black smoke. "Fire! My God! Everyone wake up!" Her cries split the night.

Olivia was the first person out, followed by the others, all plunging headlong into a living nightmare. Nora Dalton shouted above their screams and the roar of a fire being swept through the brush by a steady wind. "Someone go for the forest rangers! Todd, Olivia." She pointed to the two who were in her direct line of sight. "You're fast riders." They wasted no time getting on their bicycles and pedaling off.

The flames lapped wildly at the trees and brush, and the air was heavy with soot. Most of the kids were already battling the fire, using towels, water from their water bottles, handfuls of dirt—anything and everything to suffocate the burning leaves and branches.

"This is the end!" Lila cried in fear. "Oh, I know this is it!" She put her hands over her eyes and shrieked to the sky.

Ms. Dalton was instantly at her side. "Lila, stop. We're going to be OK. We're going to beat this fire. We'll be fine."

Lila continued to scream, her body trembling hysterically. "No! I don't want to die!"

Ms. Dalton didn't hesitate. She took Lila by the shoulders and gave her a hard shake. "Lila, snap out of it. We need every hand we can get. You have to pull yourself together!" She shook her again.

Elizabeth saw Lila push Ms. Dalton away from her with the terrified strength of someone twice her size. "What do you know about pulling yourself together anyway?" she yelled. "All you know about is messing up other people's lives and then running away!"

"Oh, Lila," Elizabeth moaned. "Not now."

But it was too late. Mr. Collins had heard every word. "Lila, she's trying to help!" he shouted.

"Oh, sure. Just like she helped her husband!"

"Husband?!" Shock registered on Roger Collins's handsome face.

"Mr. Collins, hurry!" Annie's voice rang out from behind the flames. "It's spreading like crazy!"

Mr. Collins whipped around. There was no time for anything but fighting the fire. If they waited for the rangers, it could be too late. "OK, Liz, Nora, Lila—you take that area over on the right, the one no one's covering. The rest of you, keep at the front and other side."

"Mr. Collins, what about back here, where the wind's blowing?" Bruce called. "I don't see how we're going to stop it. I can't get anywhere near the flames!"

"There's only one chance. We've got to get way behind it and cut it off—choke it. I need two volunteers who are strong enough to lift big branches and pull up shrubs. If we strip a patch bare, the fire won't have anywhere to go."

"I'm with you!" yelled Bruce.

"Me too," put in Roger.

"No way!" Bruce shouted to his cousin.

Elizabeth couldn't believe her ears. Had Bruce gone off the deep end? Of all times to rebuff Roger's efforts . . .

"No! We're not going to risk more than one Patman at a time!" he insisted. His voice had the ring of an older brother protecting a younger one. Elizabeth did an astonished about-face in her evaluation.

"Charlie and I will go," Bruce announced.

Roger didn't say a word. He never ceased beating down the fire with a large metal pan, its handle wrapped with a T-shirt to keep it from getting burning hot. His face was blackened with soot, and sweat stood out on his forehead. But in the middle of it all, as he signaled his acceptance of Bruce's decision with a swift nod, Elizabeth could see that Roger was smiling. An incredulous, joyful smile.

No one had ever heard Bruce refer to his cousin as a Patman before. This made it official. Roger was part of the family. Roger finally belonged.

It was no time for a long-awaited reunion between the cousins, however. The fire raged on, and the group fought it with every ounce of energy they possessed. Finally it began to recede on three sides. But the wind blew life into the fourth side. Somewhere behind the opaque clouds of smoke, Mr. Collins, Charlie, and Bruce were working valiantly to block its path. It crackled and sputtered. It moved swiftly, devouring everything—a ravenous monster on a course of destruction.

And then the smoke began clearing. Shouts of triumph echoed through the thinning cloud. Elizabeth and the others rushed forward, pressing the attack, until the flames had nowhere else to go. The crackling stopped. The fire was dead.

"Hooray! It's out! Congratulations!!" Shouts of

exuberance came from every direction. Bruce sheepishly extended his arm toward Roger. They shook hands.

But Elizabeth was not part of the merrymaking. She stood silently by the camp-fire bed, staring at the ash and piles of charred wood. She had helped fight the fire and had won. But now came the hard part.

Jessica found her poking around in the coals with a branch. "Liz, are you all right?"

Elizabeth steeled herself. She had to be strong.

"Jess, remember that lecture Mr. Collins gave us at the beginning of the trip about fire prevention? How anyone who wouldn't follow his rules would be asked to leave?"

Jessica nodded.

"I was the last one up tonight." Elizabeth's expression grew darker than the inky black sky. "I put out the camp fire. At least I thought I did. This fire must be my fau—"

"No!" Jessica shouted. "Don't even say it."

"It's true, Jessica." Elizabeth closed her eyes to hold back the burning tears. "It happened because of me. In the morning, I'm going back to Sweet Valley."

"Liz, you can't just leave!" wailed Jessica. "Now that Robbie's turned out to be such a disaster, I need your company. If you don't say anything, nobody has to know."

226

"Jessica, that'd be almost like lying. My mind's made up. It's the only thing to do."

"But no one was even hurt." Jessica was insistent.

"I heard Courtney saying something about all the poor animals that were probably killed."

"Oh, so now she's the very soul of responsibility. Liz, you know what that girl is really like. You don't have to listen to her!"

"Jessica, this time she's right. Please don't try to stop me." Elizabeth headed back to the rest of the group. Her back was rigid with determination. "I have to tell them. This trip is over for me."

Sixteen

"Nora, what did she mean? What was Lila saying? And what's going on with you and the kids on this trip? Everyone's acting so strangely." Roger Collins had Nora Dalton by the shoulders. "Nora, I'm begging you. Talk to me."

Nora Dalton was trembling. "Not now, Roger. Wasn't the fire enough excitement for one night?" Several yards away the group was still engaged in a noisy celebration of their victory.

"If not now, when?" Mr. Collins demanded. "You can't keep avoiding me like this."

"What difference does it make?" Ms. Dalton asked wearily. Her face was drawn, and there were dark, puffy rings around her eyes. Whatever was happening, Roger Collins could see the great toll it was taking on her. "We're through with each other. We decided that," she continued. "Why get involved with my personal problems?" Her voice was a weak whisper in the dark.

Mr. Collins shook his head sadly. "Nora, I never decided anything. You were the one who called it off between us, without ever explaining why. I was angry. I was hurt. I told myself I hated you for what you'd done to me. It was easier than admitting the truth to myself."

"Roger, no!" Nora Dalton covered her ears with her hands. "Don't do this!"

"Nora, listen!" Mr. Collins grabbed her hands. "I can't run away from it any longer, and neither can you. The other day at the ocean, when you were in trouble, it was all so clear. I still care about you, Nora Dalton. That hasn't changed, even though you say you don't return my feelings."

"Oh, Roger, if only you knew," she said softly, almost to herself.

"Knew what? Tell me. If there's something wrong, I want to help you."

"No one can help me, Roger. And you'll only get yourself in a terrible bind if you try. Stay away from me. I'm nothing but trouble."

Roger Collins gazed into Nora Dalton's sorrow-filled eyes. She was a mystery, a beautiful mystery. During those few wonderful weeks they'd been dating, she'd been so warm, so much fun. But even then, there were times when she seemed to turn inward, and a haunting, eerie sadness would claim her as its own.

"You've got to level with me," he pleaded. "What does Lila Fowler know that I don't?"

Her reply was a single shake of her brunette head. "You're a good man. You don't deserve to be a part of my problems."

"Is that it? Is that why you said you didn't want me? I'll stand by you no matter what. I believe in you."

Tears filled Nora Dalton's eyes. "You won't, if I tell you my story. No one believes in me. That's the whole trouble."

"Try me." Roger Collins never let go of her slender hands.

Nora Dalton hesitated like a frightened child on a diving board. Finally she took the plunge. "I guess you're going to hear it eventually, anyway. Who knows how many people Lila's already told. At least I can give it to you straight." She breathed deeply. "My real name is Beth Curtis . . ."

Mr. Collins listened, his initial incredulousness melting in the light of understanding, as she told him how she'd left her husband and about his subsequent suicide. She talked about his family, their wealth and power.

"They said I left him for another man, that it was my fault. They threatened to ruin my career. They made my life so miserable that I had to leave. Go someplace where I could start fresh. Where no one knew me and rumors wouldn't follow."

"And was someone else involved?" Mr. Collins asked gently. "Nora, I just can't imagine you could ever drive anyone to something so drastic."

As the smoke from the fire gave way to a breezy, clear night, Nora Dalton's eyes searched his. "You really are on my side, aren't you?"

Mr. Collins nodded encouragingly. "Why did you leave John Curtis? Nothing could be worse than keeping it inside you for so long."

"Roger, my husband was a very disturbed man. There were months when he seemed just fine—like when I first met him, for instance. But he'd had long periods of debilitating depression, drinking binges, run-ins with the law. I didn't know it when I married him, and his family never said a word. It seems they'd always covered up for him. He'd done some terrible, violent things on those binges, bar brawls and worse, much worse. It just wouldn't do for such an important family to have a problem like that. So they hid it. Even from me.

"Of course after we were married, I found out. But they figured it was too late. He was my responsibility. Now I had to take care of him, cover for him. I tried. Really, I did." Ms. Dalton choked on her words.

"Of course you did, Nora," consoled Mr. Collins. "But then something happened."

She nodded. "He came home so drunk one night he could barely get through the door. I'd been worried sick over him. I asked where he'd been. He screamed at me. He said it was none of my business. We fought and"—Nora Dalton drew her hands away from Roger Collins and covered her face—"he hit me."

Mr. Collins wrapped her in his arms. She didn't resist.

"It got worse and worse," she said sobbing. "I was so frightened. Finally I had to leave. For my own safety. John called me several days later, apologizing. He promised he'd never drink again. But he'd said that so many times before. He wanted me to come home to him. He begged me. I said no. Roger, that evening he shot himself. . . ." Nora Dalton collapsed against Roger Collins's chest.

"Why didn't you tell anyone?" Mr. Collins's voice was brimming with sympathy. He hugged her tighter.

"John's family. They said if I spilled a word of this to anyone, they'd make me wish I'd been the one who'd died." Her body was racked with sobs. Mr. Collins waited until she'd quieted down. She began speaking again. "I had no choice but to leave town."

"So you found Sweet Valley." Roger Collins's mind was whirling in confusion from Nora's story. But there was still something he didn't understand. "Why did you keep guarding your secret once you got to our town?"

"What else could I do? If the Curtises had discovered my talking about their son there—or anywhere—they would have ruined my new life, also."

"Don't you trust the people you've met in Sweet Valley, Nora? Do you really think we'd let someone destroy you?"

"It happened once. It could happen again. Besides . . ." Nora Dalton's hands vibrated with fear.

"You can tell me."

"George Fowler."

Roger Collins grew tense. He let his arms drop to his sides and took a step backward. "What about him?"

"He knows the Curtises. Does business with them. He heard the story and figured out who I was. Of course he heard their version of the story, but I was too frightened to tell him the truth. And I was terrified he'd expose my former life to the entire town of Sweet Valley."

"Blackmail!" Roger Collins's jaw dropped open in shock.

"Not exactly." Nora Dalton lowered her eyes. "He just sort of managed to take up more and more of my time. . . . Oh, what does it matter, anyway?" She was inconsolable. "Now that Lila's heard about me, my life in Sweet Valley is over. I'll have to flee again, hide."

"Nora, you can't keep running away. You have to stay and fight."

"I can't."

"Why not?"

"Roger—I can't help thinking—what if I had taken John back when he'd asked? He might be alive today."

"That's really it, isn't it?" Mr. Collins's voice softened. "You blame yourself. John's family's even got *you* believing you're guilty. Nora, no. His problems obviously went much deeper than your marriage. No one can be fully responsible for another person's life. Stop beating yourself for something you couldn't have helped. Stop running. Stay in Sweet Valley. It's your home. Stay and fight, if you have to. If your secret's out anyway, you have nothing to lose."

"Roger, I'm so scared."

"I understand. I would be, too. But I'll be by your side—if you want me to be, that is."

"Roger, I never stopped loving you," she confessed. "But George Fowler, and the whole situation—"

Roger Collins interrupted her sentence with a gentle kiss on the lips, then another one, more insistent. His heart beat wildly. "Nora, that's all over. I love you, too. Together we're going to see the end of this tragedy. You will stay, won't you?"

"For you." She kissed him again.

"No, for you," he replied.

"Yes, for me." Nora Dalton's smile was the only answer Roger Collins needed.

Elizabeth was running. She didn't know where she was heading, but she had to get away.

"Liz! Liz, wait!" Mr. Collins's voice resounded through the trees.

She kept going, crashing through the underbrush, wildly, aimlessly. She felt a strong hand on her shoulder.

"Elizabeth!" Mr. Collins was panting. "One Wakefield lost in the woods was bad enough. What's happening?"

"Mr. Collins, I can't explain it again. Go ask Jessica or Annie, or someone." She turned away; she wanted to get as far from the campsite as she could. But Mr. Collins continued to keep his hand on her shoulder. "The fire—I never got to explain why. Because Courtney—she said she and Todd. . . . Oh, please, I can't go into it. The others heard—while you and Ms. Dalton were talking— They know." Elizabeth's words tumbled out in fragmented, incohesive bursts.

"Liz, you're not making any sense." Mr. Collins took her arm. "Just calm down. We're not going anywhere until we both catch our breath and you let me in on what's happening. Liz, you're my responsibility, you know."

"Mr. Collins, please don't even say that word to me." Elizabeth wished the ground would open up and swallow her right then and there. "It was my responsibility to put the fire out, and then Courtney decided it was her responsibility to tell me she was leaving with Todd—"

"Liz, every one of us had a responsibility to pitch in and squelch that fire, and we did. It wasn't your burden alone. And what is this about your boyfriend and Courtney? I'm your friend. You can talk to me."

"Mr. Collins, Todd is not my boyfriend!"

"He's not?" Mr. Collins was shocked. "Liz, I admit, I've been a bit preoccupied recently, and you have seemed, well, at odds with your usual good spirits, but I didn't know. . . . Why didn't you tell me?" The astonishment on his face was clear. And it was no surprise. Elizabeth and Todd had been the first to agree when people said they were a perfect couple.

Even as she unfolded all the sorry events to Mr. Collins, Elizabeth could barely believe them herself. When she got to the most recent part, she felt almost as if she were watching a movie about another girl altogether. "I approached the group to tell them how the fire was my fault, but Courtney was already talking to them, explaining that she'd be leaving the trip and that Todd was going with her, to be her guest for the rest of the summer!" Her words sounded hollow to her own ears. There was no more crying, no more running. Only an empty space inside her.

Mr. Collins let out a long, heavy sigh. "If I weren't living through this night, I'd say it wasn't possible."

"Mr. Collins?"

"Elizabeth, I just finished talking to Ms. Dalton about how you can't solve your problems by running away from them. You might be able to learn something from her story." He told Elizabeth about John Curtis and his family and everything Nora Dalton had tried to leave behind.

"Poor Ms. Dalton!" exclaimed Elizabeth. "Of course she has to tell everyone the real story. They've *got* to believe her."

"So you agree she should stay and fight?"

"Of course." Elizabeth nodded.

"Liz, right now, she's telling the story I just told you to all your tripmates." Mr. Collins waved his arm in the direction of the campsite. "That's not an easy thing to do, but she loves Sweet Valley, and she wants it to be her home. So she has to stand up for herself, or she might lose what she wants so badly. Do you understand?"

"I understand about Ms. Dalton, but what does it have to do with me?"

"Do you love Todd, Liz?"

Elizabeth swallowed hard. "I'm pretty upset with him right now, but, yes, I do."

"Then you have to stand up for yourself. Don't run away. You won't win him back that way."

"But Mr. Collins, Courtney needs him more than I do."

"Now *I'm* the one who doesn't understand."

"Her father, his drinking, the whole reason she was sent on this trip!" As she related the details, she noticed a glimmer of understanding spreading across Roger Collins's chiseled features. "Mr. Collins, what is it?"

"Liz, tell me something. Do you believe that story?"

Elizabeth raised her shoulders. She felt like a toy boat lost in a vast sea of confusion and despair. "I don't even know. First I didn't, then I did, then I didn't again. I can't decide anymore."

"I don't believe in breaking confidences," Roger Collins began. "But in this case, I don't think I have much choice. I hope Steve Thomas will forgive me."

"Mr. Thomas?" questioned Elizabeth.

"Yes. There's not a thing wrong with him, Elizabeth. But there is quite a lot wrong with his daughter and her friends. Especially everyone's favorite, Nolan Ruggers." The moonlight was reflected in Mr. Collins's serious blue eyes. Elizabeth listened as he told her about the stealing and the drugs. "Courtney seems to have a number of different versions about why she was sent on this trip. But the real one is that Steve Thomas wanted his daughter as far from Nolan Ruggers as he could get her."

Elizabeth felt her sadness and confusion vanishing like morning dew in the sun. "Then Todd—"

Mr. Collins nodded. "She must be using him for her own scheme. I imagine Todd would be a signal to her father that she's mended her ways. He'd let her come home—where Nolan would be right around the corner."

"Mr. Collins, I've got to find Todd! If I can convince him, everything will be just the way it—" Elizabeth stopped in midsentence, her mouth turning down again. "But of course it won't be. The fire—I'll still be going home tomorrow."

Mr. Collins's jaw was tight. "Liz, it would be untrue if I said everything would be OK. The fire business is a serious situation. If you really were the last one out—"

"I was," Elizabeth affirmed.

"Elizabeth, I want you to know you're more than just one of my favorite students. I consider you a friend."

"But rules are rules," Elizabeth finished.

"Look, I'm going to have to discuss this with Ms. Dalton. It'll be hard to see you go." Mr. Collins stared at the ground. Suddenly he looked up again. "But, meanwhile, Liz, don't give up on Todd. Fight for what you want! Don't let one thing get in the way of the other!"

Elizabeth nodded her head. It wouldn't be quite so bad to leave the trip knowing she'd finally set things straight with Todd. She no longer felt like running away. Now she had a direction. She knew exactly what she had to do.

* * *

"I guess I never realized how many friends I've already made in Sweet Valley." Nora Dalton's pretty face glowed in the moonlight.

"We're all right behind you, Ms. Dalton," said Annie.

Elizabeth sensed the unspoken bond between her French teacher and her beautiful friend. Annie Whitman knew better than anyone else what it was like to fight ugly rumors. Now Annie's encouraging smile and her head on Charlie's shoulder showed that she had won. And Nora Dalton's hopeful, determined expression made it clear that she intended to do the same.

"Lila," she said, "it was especially hard for me to say all this in front of you."

Lila toyed with a loose thread on her sweater. "OK, so it did take courage," she admitted, not looking up.

"Thank you, Lila," Ms. Dalton returned graciously.

"We're very proud of you, Nora." Mr. Collins went around to where she sat and draped his arm around her shoulder. "Each and every one of us."

Elizabeth cleared her throat nervously. She caught Mr. Collins's eye. He gave a gentle smile and nodded his head. "As long as we're clearing things up," she began, "I have something else to air, and I think Courtney does, too." At the edge of the gathering, Elizabeth could see Todd. He and Olivia had just shaken hands with the forest rangers and were bidding them good night.

"What do you mean, Liz?" Courtney demanded. "Are you talking about my leaving? Todd and me, that is. Everyone already knows about that."

Elizabeth watched Todd move closer. "No, Courtney. I'm talking about why you're taking Todd with you. That, and the real reason why your father sent you on this trip." Elizabeth tried to keep her voice strong. It wasn't in her nature to fight like this, but she knew it was her only hope. She also knew that she was matching wits with a pro.

"Liz, you've heard the reason!" Todd's voice pierced the tense air. "How can you make Courtney talk about it, when you know how much it'll hurt? It's not fair to her or her father."

"Todd, Courtney is one good storyteller. But that's all she's been telling you—mixed-up, made-up stories. If you want to talk about fair, it's only fair that Courtney let you in on the truth." Elizabeth gathered steam as her emotions welled inside her.

"Liz, this is a private matter." Elizabeth could hear the anger just under the surface of Courtney's words. All she had to do was push a little more, and Courtney's veneer of sweetness would melt like cotton candy in the rain.

"It's no longer a private matter when your lies start ruining my vacation," she challenged.

"I know what your problem is, Elizabeth Wakefield." Courtney clenched her fists, her knuckles white, her teeth bared. "You're just jealous because Todd's going with me instead of staying here with you!"

"That's where you're wrong Courtney." Elizabeth shook her head sadly. "I'm leaving, too."

"What?" Several astonished voices rang out.

"I'm afraid that's what I had to level with all of you about," Elizabeth began. "You see, I was the last one out tonight. It was my responsibility to put out the campfire. I guess I didn't do a good enough job." She hung her head.

"Aw, Liz," said Barry. Annie Whitman looked as though she was close to tears.

"Wait just a minute!" Todd's baritone rang out. "You weren't the last one out." A strange expression was crossing his face, as if he'd just taken a sip of sour milk.

Courtney sprang to life again. "Todd!" There was a warning in the way she spoke his name.

"I don't believe this," murmured Todd.

"Don't believe what?" asked Olivia, standing by his side.

Todd looked Courtney straight in the eye. Then he turned to Elizabeth. "Courtney and I were out after you." He paused uncomfortably. "And Courtney was smoking a cigarette!"

"That's a lie!" As Courtney screamed, Elizabeth could see her mask fall away.

"But, Courtney," protested Todd, "I saw you flip your butt into those bushes. . . ." His sentence trailed off as comprehension colored his face. The bushes he pointed to were where the fire had raged the hardest.

Courtney turned pale. "What difference does it make, anyway? I don't need to be subjected to all these accusations. Let's go, Todd. There must be some way to get out of this place before morning."

"No!" Todd's refusal rang out. "I'm not going anywhere," he said. A light had just gone on in his head. "I'm starting to wonder why I agreed to leave with you in the first place. Everything I want is right here." He looked at Elizabeth and gave a hesitant smile. "How could I have been so blind?"

Elizabeth's voice was low. "I guess a lot of people were fooled."

"Liz, 'I'm sorry' isn't enough. God, what I've put you through. . . ." Shame colored Todd's face. "I wouldn't blame you if you never wanted to see me again. But, please," he said, his gaze never leaving Elizabeth's face, "if nothing else, believe me when I tell you that I never meant to hurt you. I love you so much."

Elizabeth smiled, tentatively at first, then with more certainty. She stretched her hand out toward Todd. He took it in both of his.

"Bravo!" Jessica shouted and began to applaud.

"Well, you can just keep your wonderful Elizabeth!" Courtney yelled out. "I'm glad you don't want to come with me. Saves me from telling you that I've changed my mind. You're nothing but—but—" She spat on the ground. "That's what you are. And Elizabeth, too." Courtney moved closer to them, and they turned toward her. "You know what? You two deserve each other."

A giggle escaped Elizabeth's lips, followed by another. Soon it was full-fledged laughter, with Todd joining in. "You know, Courtney," Elizabeth managed, "for once I couldn't agree with you more!"

Seventeen

"That's when the fun really began," Elizabeth told her best friend, Enid Rollins. The group had gotten home the night before, and now she and Enid were sitting in lounge chairs by the Wakefield pool, catching up on everything the summer had brought. "It was as if the sun had finally come out from behind a huge cloud."

Enid nodded thoughtfully. "It's funny how it took the two worst disasters—Jessica's bear and the fire—to bring everyone together."

"Mmm. Thank goodness for that. You know Todd could have been in Beverly Hills right now."

"And instead, Courtney got sent to her aunt's?"

"Mr. Collins put her on the early-morning bus out of Santa Cruz. I almost feel sorry for her." Elizabeth trailed her fingers in the pool.

"I wouldn't, Liz." Enid shook her head.

"She's probably finding some way to make trouble there, too. And speaking of trouble, what ended up happening to your sister and Lila?"

Elizabeth laughed. "Oh, they met these two Frisbee players from the University of Santa Cruz. After that, they suddenly became the biggest Frisbee freaks this side of the Rockies. Not for long, though. They were playing on the beach right next to one of the hostels we were staying in, and Jessica managed to put the Frisbee right through one of the windows. She had to pay for it out of her pocket money. After that, I guess she decided boy chasing was a cheaper sport."

Enid's green eyes sparkled as she laughed. "And Lila?"

"Oh, Lila gave it up, too. She and Jess started competing over guys instead!"

"No more Robbie, huh?"

"Oh, my gosh, Enid. That's the best part! We saw him once more—on the road. His brother had gotten a flat tire, and neither of them knew how to fix it! So—you won't believe this one—Barry did it for them!" Elizabeth giggled. "But then, when we were in San Francisco, having dinner in Chinatown, Barry spilled hot-and-sour soup all over about half the group! I guess some things never change."

"Except Bruce Patman," Enid said. "Liz, it's

still hard for me to believe he turned out to be such a pussycat."

"Well, don't expect to see anything but the same old tiger on the outside," Elizabeth warned. "I think he's still kind of embarrassed about letting us see his soft side. But, Enid, what about you? Who's this guy you wrote me about? Hank, is it?"

Enid blushed. "He was visiting from Boston. His grandparents live here. It took him three straight days of coming in and ordering chocolate-chip cones before he worked up enough nerve to ask me out! We promised to write to each other."

"I bet it was hard to see the summer ending," Elizabeth remarked wistfully.

"It did go by awfully fast," Enid replied.

"I know exactly how you feel." Elizabeth's blond ponytail bobbed up and down as she nodded. "Time just seemed to fly by. I wish I could do it all over again. Well, not exactly all of it, but—you know—all the good parts."

"Oh, you mean like making up with Todd?" Enid teased, raising her eyebrows suggestively.

Elizabeth leaned over, dipped her hand into the pool, and sent a splash of water in her friend's direction.

Enid squealed and turned her head away. "Just telling it like it is," she said, giggling.

"Well, for that matter," Elizabeth replied, "I'll bet *you* wouldn't mind repeating the day that a certain someone from Boston came into Casey's and ordered his first ice-cream cone from you!"

Enid leaned forward, swirled a cupped hand through the water, and brought it up in a counterattack. "You may be right, Liz, but you're all wet!" She let out a peal of laughter.

Elizabeth jumped up and grabbed the back of Enid's lounge chair. "You're going to be sorry, Rollins!" She tipped the chair toward the pool's glimmering surface.

"No, Liz!" Enid pleaded, scurrying to her feet before she toppled in. "Now what kind of way is that to treat someone you haven't seen all summer?" she said, laughing. "You're supposed to give me a big hug instead. Like this." Enid stood up and threw her arms around Elizabeth. Suddenly she pulled her toward the water.

Caught off balance, Elizabeth felt herself falling in, but not before firmly grasping Enid's hand. They both hit the water at the same time, shrieking and sputtering water.

The two friends resurfaced loudly. "Tie?" Elizabeth asked.

"Tie," Enid agreed. "And, Liz, it's great to have you home again."

Elizabeth looked at Enid's smiling face and then at the Wakefields' comfortable familiar house. From upstairs came the sounds of Jessica's stereo. Downstairs through the glass doors that opened onto the patio, Elizabeth could see her parents reading the Sunday paper.

She knew that Steven was inside watching something on TV. "Know what, Enid?" Elizabeth said. "As perfect as the summer turned out, I still missed Sweet Valley and all of you. I'm glad to be back, too."

Caitlin

From Francine Pascal, the creator of the SWEET VALLEY HIGH® books, comes something new and very exciting. It's CAITLIN: A LOVE TRILOGY and you won't want to miss it!

Caitlin — she's gorgeous, charming, rich and a little wild; she's the outrageous, dazzling star of LOVING, LOVE LOST, and TRUE LOVE. You're going to want to read all three —just to see what Caitlin will do next as she reaches out for her heart's desire!

For readers who like lots of excitement with their romance and lots of romance with their excitement — CAITLIN: A LOVE TRILOGY! Get it wherever paperback books are sold!

Bantam Books